RAVAGE MC BOUND SERIES BOOK ONE

BOUND
BY *Family*

RYAN MICHELE

1ˢᵗ edition published: March 28, 2017
Editing by: C&D Editing
Proofread: Silla Webb
Cover Design by: Cassy Roop at Pink Ink Designs
Photography by: Wander Aguiar
Models: Jamie Walker and Tiffany Marie

DEDICATION

To my sinners, without you, this story would have never come to life.
Thank you for helping me find my happy again.
Love always, Ryan

TABLE OF CONTENTS

PROLOGUE
Cooper

This life.

My life … is Ravage.

Some say it's my destiny. Others call this my curse.

Lucky for me, I don't give a fuck what anyone thinks. The man I've become is because of a choice—none of that other bullshit. Everyone in life has a choice, a path. What direction you take is up to you.

For me, I had this moment in my life, a moment when I knew who and what I'd become.

It wasn't forced or coerced as the talk has been around this small town. No, the moment that haunts my dreams is what created the man you see today.

Family.

From the beginning to the end, family is what you start with and what you end with. I'm bound to it, honored by it, and respected in it.

RYAN MICHELE

CHAPTER ONE
Cooper

The echo of the hammer hitting bone crackles through the air in the small, dank room. The man's screams fill the space with pain, anger, and contempt. He doesn't want us here anymore than we want to be in this dump. Unfortunately for us both, he fucked up and it isn't an option. No, it's a necessity.

Fucking Stu.

Ravage Motorcycle Club, my family, we run a tight ship, so to speak. There is a code, rules of sorts that must be followed. Fall out of line, there will be punishment. Stu fell out of line.

Ryker laughs off to the side, pulling me away from my thoughts as I let go of the man's wrist, hammer still clenched in the other hand. The asshole, Stu, falls to his knees on the dirt floor, holding his broken finger.

That's not the only one he's going to get today for his stupidity.

He knows better. Everyone in Sumner, Georgia knows better. Hell, make that anyone who has ever heard of Ravage knows better.

"You've got a hell of a blow with that thing," Ryker calls out. The man is twisted and warped. He does this shit for fun and entertainment. Part of me thinks he gets off on it, but to each their own. Me, I do this shit out of duty and responsibility. Regardless, he's been by my side for years, and I wouldn't have it any other way.

When no response comes from me, Ryker walks up to the man and gives him a savage kick to the gut, making the man curl into a ball to protect himself. Green and Jacks stand off to the side of the small space.

We brought Stu to one of our outbuildings. It's more like a rundown shack, but it has what we need to get the job done.

"I'm thinkin' we need to take off some piggies," Ryker eggs on, and a chuckle escapes me. He does have a way with words, saying exactly what he thinks with not an ounce of filter.

"Give me a shot," Jacks, another one of my brothers and a friend from high school, says as he holds his hand out to me, waiting for the hammer.

Handing it to him, I then take a step back and cross my arms. It's not me being a pussy. It's me wanting to get this shit done so we can get the fuck out of here.

"Money," I bark out to Stu as Ryker gives him another hard kick, this one to his thigh.

Stu owes our club fifty thousand seven hundred dollars and some change for merchandise he purchased. We gave him a week after the initial payment of fifty grand went smooth. Ravage and Stu have a history, and in that time, this is the first instance when Stu hasn't paid up in full. It'll be the last time as well.

"I-I can have it b-by the weekend," Stu stammers out as Jacks swings the hammer, hitting Stu in the ankle. Another crunching sound reverberates throughout the room.

Ryker smirks, coming to stand next to me and giving me a slight bump on the shoulder with his elbow. "Believe this fucker? Weekend?" He shakes his head and spits down at Stu. "Motherfucker, you have twenty-four hours to come up with the cash."

"If we don't have it by then, you're done," I add as Jacks takes another swing.

His cries of fear fill the air.

After an hour of making sure Stu gets the picture by using our fists and hammer, we ride.

Fresh air. The freedom of feeling the elements surround me. The delicate balance of navigating a road or eating asphalt.

It's the best part of every day.

The ride.

My bike is a beauty. A Heritage Softtail Harley painted black and red—Ravage MC colors. Working on her has been my pastime for years, tuning and cleaning. I take care of her, and she takes care of me. Wouldn't have it any other way. There's something about taking garbage and turning it into something you love. That's my bike. She began as a pile of shit and turned out to be absolutely perfect.

Life ties us down. Materials hold people back. The open road is about freedom. Ravage is freedom. We live to our code, our standards, and we take care of our own.

My mind clears on the open road awaiting me, nothing but blacktop and paint ahead. Riding allows me the peaceful time to think. Sometimes my rides last hours, while others only last minutes. Normally, whenever my mind figures out what it needs to, that's the time I pull my bike to a stop.

Lately, the Ravage MC has been bringing in some serious money with all the deals that Pops has worked out over the years. Some of them bring more than others, but it's becoming more difficult to filter the money. Especially with the amount of cash. There's only so much we can put through the garage and Studio X, the strip club. Even Stu owes us, and when that cash shows up … Well, it's got to go somewhere.

It's been working well, but we had to stock pile cash in several of our vaults in the clubhouse basement. Having cash on hand is great in the times we need it, but it will continually increase over time if we keep at this pace. That being said, we need something else to funnel the money.

The thing is, I've been around the club my whole life. I prospected in early. Just turning twenty-two, I've held my place for four years now. I'm ready to step up anywhere needed. More so, I'm ready to give a fresh mindset and view to the way we do business. It's all for family.

My Ravage family.

My top idea is a car wash. It's an all-cash business, unless you let the customers use credit cards, which I would advise against. If we keep it all cash, we could put some of the money through there. I even searched the internet about all the working parts of one of the machines and how much it would take to build and maintain it. Ravage could easily do it, but the downside is all the moving pieces. Sure, we can go and fix the shit, but I want to work smarter, not harder.

There's a way, and I will damn well find it.

My parents taught me many things. The first and foremost is to be my own man. If that means carving a new path for the Ravage MC, I'm up to the task.

Pulling up to the clubhouse, we park in the lot, all next to each other, turning off the engines and taking off our helmets.

This building is home.

My memory is damn good, which is both a blessing and a curse. My father doesn't know, but I remember living with my biological mother and seeing stuff as a young child that was flat-out wrong. It's not that he doesn't care to know; we just don't talk about it.

Besides, remembering those times only pisses me off. Seeing men come in and out of the small apartment, going into that woman's bedroom then coming out a while later. She was always doped up on something. Back then, I thought she just wasn't feeling well.

When she started hitting me, that was when I knew what fear was. A woman is supposed to love their kid, at least somewhat. Mine didn't. Not at all.

The moment my father told that woman—my incubator, as we call her now—I was staying with him, that's what I consider my rebirth. It was a new start. Not only that, but I had a new mother, as well. One who loved me, took care of me, and put all my needs above anyone else's, not giving two shits what anyone thought about it.

When I started living, this ugly-as-fuck, cement-blocked building became home. Don't get me wrong, we had a house, as well, but the clubhouse is where it all started for me.

"How'd it go?" Pops, the president of Ravage MC and my grandfather, asks upon us entering the building as I get chin lifts from the guys.

Pops has been the president since I came to Ravage—at least eighteen years. He's done a great job building the Ravage Motorcycle Club into very profitable entities. Not only that, after the bullshit that went down when I was a kid, Pops keeps a tight leash on any and all our friends and enemies. One doesn't do what we do and not have a huge basket of both, but Pops has kept it all in line.

"Ryker got a little too happy, so the guy won't be having kids, probably ever, but the message was sent. If he doesn't have it by the weekend, then we'll take care of it."

Pops chuckles.

"Hey, the fucker was tryin' to stand up. If he would've stayed down, his nuts wouldn't have cracked."

Laughter is heard throughout the clubhouse.

Pops slaps his hand on my shoulder, giving it a squeeze. The look he gives me is different, but he says nothing as he walks to one of the tables and has a seat.

I've noticed things about him these last few months. The looks that come across his face when he thinks no one is looking, as if he's tired and the weight of the world rests on his shoulders. There's no doubt in my mind that it's true.

Running an entire MC is a shit-ton of work. Even doing it for years and having it down pat, there comes a time when it could be too much. I kept my mouth shut about it, though, not wanting to overstep my boundaries. When Pops is ready to tell us what's going on, he will.

Heading toward the bar, I grasp the cold beer sitting on it then join the guys at the table. Blood means nothing to any of us. We are a family of our own choosing. Each one of us couldn't be more different if we tried. It's as if we were put together in this clubhouse for a reason.

Take Becs. He's the vice president and has recently told us that he'd like to step down and let one of the younger guys take his role. That decision is huge and one of the highest topics at our next church. Becs is quiet. Silent but deadly. He's never up in your face, but one wrong move, and he will tear you down.

Then there's Rhys. He's silent, but his face, body—hell, even the air around him—screams "breath my air, and I'll end you."

My dad, Cruz, he's middle road between the two. He has no problem getting in someone's face, yet he'll only do it when necessary. His face isn't scary like Rhys', but he has his own badass vibe he puts off.

Me, I'm more of a thinker, a planner if you will. I like to look at all the possibilities and facts before coming up with a strategy.

Somehow, all our crazy asses fit together, and we are bound by family.

CHAPTER TWO
Cooper

Watching from a chair by the fire pit, I bring the beer to my lips and drink. The party boy sits over at the picnic table in the open area of grass next to the clubhouse, head hanging down like he's deep in thought. I remember being in the exact same position on more than one occasion.

Growing up, I was alone except when other charters of Ravage came and brought their children. We'd have fun, and then they left, creating the same vicious cycle over and over again. Then Deke was born, and all I wanted to do was play with him.

Even though he was an infant, I was ready to play cars or hide and seek—anything. Once he got to an age where he could keep up with me, we were tight like brothers, even though we are technically cousins. It seems like so long ago because so much has changed.

Being so much older than most of my generation of the Ravage MC children, I feel as if I skipped a level now that I'm a brother.

The younger children play, laugh, and run around like crazy, screaming with excitement. They must've had too much sugar with all the energy they have, which doesn't surprise me, considering my grandma, otherwise known as Ma in the club, made enough cake to feed double our family. Not to mention, the cookies and fudge she added because they are Deke's favorites. She's always been great about making sure we all have what we need when we need it.

The sun shines bright with a nice breeze. It's a perfect day to go for a ride after this is over. Judging from Deke's pissed off attitude as he sits stewing, it'll be over sooner rather than later. He hasn't said a word, but I know exactly why he's pissed. The party's coming to an end and Pops never called him in. He's not going to, either.

There were no second thoughts in me joining the club. I had a plan when I turned eighteen—to prospect and earn my cut. No questions asked. Pops and the brothers broke tradition and gave me my leather on my sixteenth birthday.

Normally, one would have to wait until they're eighteen to start prospecting. Then, in a year or two, if the brothers voted unanimously to let you in, you were in. One "no" vote meant you were out; couldn't remain a prospect any longer and had zero affiliation with the club. You were gone.

Today is Deke's sixteenth birthday, and he wanted the cut to bring him into the fold just like I got on mine. Us brothers talked about it in church, and my uncle, GT, Deke's father, said Deke's not ready for this. Therefore, Deke has to wait until the time is right for him.

I thought my teen years were a little on the wild side, but Deke's are a bit over the charts. Not that it's bad, but Deke needs to learn to reign it in. There's a time for partying and a time for serious shit.

My mother, Princess, says Deke is worse than GT when he was younger. GT is her brother. My mom said, *"That boy is too much like his father. He needs to get his shit together."* Good thing for GT, he did. However, Deke's not there. Hopefully, he'll turn it around.

Deke thinks he's hot shit. At least, that's how he struts around here. He always has, but as he's gotten older, it's gotten worse. I can only imagine what he's like at school. It's what led to the decision not to give him his cut early. He needs to get his grades up, according to GT, and his head out of his ass, according to Pops. Being in the club isn't about status. It's about honor, loyalty, and having people there who will have your back no matter what. Deke hasn't realized that yet.

With my hand wrapped around a beer, I make my way over to the table where Deke is and sit on top of it, my steel-toed boots resting on the bench next to Deke.

Deke looks up at me. "What?" His tone is clipped and angry. It surprises me that the kid hasn't gotten up and hit something yet. His whole body vibrates with tension, like a hum of electricity ready to snake out and bite you at any given moment.

"Calm your shit. Your family did something nice for you. Don't be an asshole." I lift the beer to my lips, letting the cold brew cool my body.

The worry for Deke sits hard in my gut. He's not on the right path. He veered off somewhere, and the where is uncertain at this point.

"Go the fuck away."

I kick his thigh hard with the toe of my boot, peering down at him though my shades. The disrespectful little shit knows better than to talk to anyone here like that. His line is getting thinner by the moment.

"Watch how you talk. Don't make me pound your ass on your birthday."

He shakes his head and looks at his hands on the table, saying nothing. He's smart; that's not his problem. It's his maturity that's lacking.

Being a brother in Ravage is something you must have a clear head about. It's not just parties and rides. This is a business, as well. We have to trust each other and have each other's back at any cost. Deke doesn't have that reliability yet. Maybe in a couple of years, he'll find it ... or not.

"Deke! Come on, let's go do something," my brother, Nox, says from over by the fire pit, making his way to us.

Nox, short for Lennox, is fourteen-years-old, along with his twin sister, Austyn. He has the makings to be in the club, but he's got some years to go before that's even an option.

"What?" Deke barks a bit too hard for my liking, but I sit this out and wait. One thing I learned while being with the club is patience ... for the most part. Some things trip my trigger, but I can keep myself in check. Fighting my kid brother's battles when he's more than capable of it isn't a reason for me to go off cold-cocked.

Nox and Deke were pretty close growing up. They both got in hot water for different shit they pulled. Stupid kid things that really are a rite of passage. I admit, though, when they got together and stole a car, then spray-painted it with hot pink lettering, that was over the line, being that it was the school's principal's car. My parents and Deke's parents, GT and Angel, blew up all over both their asses. Nox and Deke were on bathroom duty in the clubhouse for four months. That's a job no one here wants, not ever.

"Let's go to the lake or something," Nox says with hope in his eyes.

"I don't want to go to the damn lake. I'm going to hang out with my friends after I leave here."

"Can I come?"

"Hell no. You're fourteen."

Nox's shoulders slump just a touch, then rise quickly. One thing I have to say about my little brother is, he may be fourteen, but he holds his own.

"What? Now that you're sixteen, you're too good for me?" he charges back, and I try to hold back a smirk.

"Damn right." Deke looks at me then back at Nox.

Thinking back, I did the same thing. Once I had the freedom of my own car, Deke and I didn't hang out like we did before. Maybe that's where his animosity comes from.

"Don't be a dickhead," Nox retaliates. "Just because you didn't—"

Deke jumps to his feet and punches my brother in the face, knocking him to the ground.

I rise from the picnic table as Deke looms over him, pointing his finger in my brother's face. "You need to keep your fucking mouth shut."

Nox rises and wipes the blood from his lip, spitting it on the ground. With fiery anger burning in his eyes, he gives Deke a savage kick to the gut, then a punch to the face. Then Nox says in a low threatening voice, now pointing his finger at Deke, "Remember who you're dealing with. I may be fourteen, but you putting your hands on me isn't going to happen."

Deke rises to his feet as brothers, their ol' ladies, and the children begin to come over to see what the fuss is about.

I hold up one hand and get chin lifts in response. These two need to work their shit out, and it's not to a point yet for anyone to step in.

"Screw you!" Deke says, lifting his fist as Nox backs up just out of reach, and Deke loses his footing.

Nox doesn't attempt to hit him back. Instead, he stands there, watching and waiting. That right there, that simple thing, is why I respect my little brother. He has skill and tact, even at his age. It also shows where Deke is lacking. Sometimes patience will win the war. Deke's half-cocked and ready to pounce rather than wait his opponent out. That, right there, will get you killed.

"What the fuck is going on here?" My mother comes up behind some of the guys and eyeballs the action just as Deke tries and fails to land another punch. "Told you, you should have practiced more, Deke. You forget; I taught my kids everything they know."

Shocking the shit out of me, she doesn't intervene. My mother is notorious for finishing fights, even if she didn't start them, just for the pure fun of it. She's something. I'm still trying to figure out what that is. Only thing I do know is she's a kickass mother who loves her kids hard and has high expectations for us. Not to mention, she lets them be voiced as much as possible.

Nox again does nothing, simply stands alert and ready. "Why do you have to be such a dick?" he asks.

Deke looks around at the crowd, then charges my brother, knocking him to the ground. Fists fly, grunts echo, and blood appears on their skin. Everyone watches. I have no doubt someone is going to jump in there pretty soon.

This teenage quarrel is just a day in the life of one of our family gatherings. Most of the time, it doesn't get this far, but Deke now has something to prove with Nox's little throw down. He wants his cut and doesn't want to be seen as a pussy in front of the guys. This is what happens when you raise a group of strong-willed kids together. There are bound to be disputes.

Each of the two take hits as I see my father and GT stand off to the side, arms crossed as they watch the chaos.

My brother somehow maneuvers Deke to his stomach with him on top. Deke's arm is extended as Nox holds it down. Deke tries to get free, but my brother holds his own. They're a pretty even body match, even with the two-year age difference.

"Alright, enough," my father calls out in that tone that makes everyone around him listen and take notice.

My dad has been with Ravage for years. He met my mother here when she got out of prison. My mom is club through and through, and if that means she had to do time for some shit she wasn't even guilty of for the club, she would do it again. It's a long story for a later time.

Nox looks up at our father, nods once, and stands up, moving away from Deke. Deke spits out curse words, no doubt feeling like an ass as he stands up.

Just as he's about to charge again, he halts at his mother's voice.

"Deacon Alexander Gavelson!" Angel yells, marching through the grass. GT gives a slight chuckle. "What the hell?"

Deke's eyes are on my brother, nostrils flaring, the animosity still burning bright. This is definitely not over.

"We're going home," Angel announces, walking up to Deke and grabbing his arm. He rips it out of her grasp, and she gives off a gasp as she steps back from the force.

When GT comes up, Deke's face remains pensive, but the small twitch in his left eye tells me he's scared shitless. He should be. GT's a fierce motherfucker, and he sure as hell won't let anyone disrespect his woman, especially not his own kids.

"Show's over," GT tells the crowd then marches Deke to the car they just bought him for his birthday that I doubt very highly he'll be driving anytime soon.

GT shoves Deke in the passenger seat, slams the door, gets in the driver's seat, and speeds off.

"Well, hell, that can't be good. Nox, come with me," my mother says.

Nox looks at our father, who lifts his chin, and then follows Mom into the clubhouse.

"Never a dull moment." Ryker clasps me on the shoulder, laughing, a cigarette hanging out of his mouth.

He patched in with Ravage a couple of years before I did, and we got pretty tight since I joined officially three, almost four, years ago.

"Such is life." Giving a shrug, I turn toward him. "What's the plan?"

He inhales then blows out the smoke. "I don't give a shit. One of the brunettes wants me to meet up with her later, but the bitch is getting too needy, and I need to cut her off." He's referring to one of the club mommas who hangs around. Their names all seem to intermingle after a while. Sex with them is release, plain and simple. There's no emotional attachment, no relationships, or any of that.

Don't get me wrong, I respect them, but I have yet to find one who I want to change that outlook for. I'm not looking for anything more than to get off. As soon as one of them thinks there'll be more, she's out.

"I'm ridin' for a while."

Ryker crosses his arms, tattoos splaying. He gets closer then opens his mouth, baring his teeth while moving his head back and forth.

I step back. "What the fuck are you doin'?"

He chuckles. "Checkin' my teeth. Those mirrored shades you wear are perfect for it."

"Asshole. You just wish you could pull this shit off."

"Nah, I'm hot enough."

I laugh. Ryker is definitely comic relief.

"Coop?" I hear my sister call as she walks up to us. Her eyes are on Ryker, though, and not me.

Austyn's had a thing for Ryker for years now, and I wish she'd get the hell over it. He's about nine or ten years older than her, so it's not happening. Hell, even if they were close in age, it still wouldn't happen. I love Ryker, but that shit's not cool with me.

"Yeah?" I ask.

She sweeps her long, dark hair behind her ear, her big blue eyes coming to me. I fully admit she's pretty, and I've seen more than one guy stop and pay her attention, but no fucking way.

"Dad wants to see you," she tells me before glancing back over at Ryker.

"Hey, little one." He ruffles her hair.

Her fists clench and shoulders tense. "Hey," she growls before stomping off, running her hand through her hair.

I just shake my head and move into the clubhouse. Either Ryker is blind or is damn good at ignoring it. Either way, I'm good with the way he's playing it.

When darkness fills my vision, I remove my sunglasses, hanging them on the front of my shirt.

My mom sits next to Nox, and I hear, "Make sure to bend the wrist back," as I walk by. Only our mother would teach better maneuvers after a fight while she's patching up a bloody lip and chin.

My dad sits at the bar, beer in hand as I walk up to him. "What's up?" I sidle up on the barstool next to him. Riley, who's prospecting, hands me a beer, and I take a heavy pull.

"Your mom and I are going away this weekend. Need you to watch over the twins."

The bottle stills on its way to my lips. "You're shitting me." His raised brow tells me he's not. I love the little shits, but that doesn't mean I want to babysit them. "They're fourteen; can't you just leave them home alone?"

"Only need you Sunday morning until we get back. Ma's going to stay over at the house Friday night, Saturday during the day, and Saturday night. Need you to take over when she leaves."

"Again, can't you leave them home alone?"

He turns his whole body toward me. "No, I can't fuckin' leave them home alone." Dad just went into the danger zone with his words. I know I need to back up a bit. I don't want to, but that's what family does.

"Fine. What time do I need to be there?"

"Nine"—his eyes don't leave mine—"in the fuckin' morning. I don't give a shit if you don't sleep Saturday night; your ass better be in my house Sunday at nine."

Great. Just fucking great.

CHAPTER THREE

Bristyl

Frustration hits me in the gut as my eyes sweep all the figures on the spreadsheet then to the little adding machine, pulling out the roll of paper and looking at them again. The numbers aren't adding up. I did them four damn times and got four different answers.

"Bristyl, what's goin' on?" my father, Regg, asks from the doorway of the office.

I rub my hands over my face, letting out a groan. He's stoic like he often is. My father is a rock of solid strength for me, for my brothers, and for his motorcycle club, Sinister Sons.

"Same old shit. Trying to get everything to iron out." Even keeping the laundromats and storage units separate, sometimes people write out of the wrong checkbook, and I have to figure it out.

The "people" I'm referring to are my brothers. I have three older ones who are a pain in my ass. Literally. They do this all the fucking time, along with not giving me their receipts. I'm over it. A woman can only take so much.

"Who did what?" he asks, taking a seat in front of my desk.

"Hunter wrote a check for the new water heater out of the unit account. Then Racer wrote one for gravel out of the laundromat account. Each of them are wrong. Not to mention, they didn't put the prices they paid, and I had to call the bank to get them. Then I had to talk to the bank again because I didn't get receipts for some things and needed to know what went where so I could get everything to balance."

"But everything's straight?" he questions with a crinkle of his forehead.

My dad is a handsome man. I'm biased, of course, but I don't give a shit. He's a hunk, meaning he's bulky as hell. When he wraps his thick, tattooed arms around me, I feel so damn little inside them. His hair is silver, along with his mustache that runs above his lip, down both sides of his mouth, and down to below his chin. He's had this look for as long as I can remember. It's all him, and I wouldn't want him any other way, even if he's been a little off lately. I just haven't figured out why.

"I really wish you'd impose the rule that they have to get the checks from me, or at least give me a receipt when they're done."

He says nothing, just stares at me, waiting for an answer to his question.

I blow out a frustrated breath. "Yes, everything'll be fine. I just need to work this out."

He rises from his chair. "We'll work it out." That's what he always says. Then, when it's time for me to do the books, I have a clusterfuck because my brothers can't keep their shit together. It's a never-ending vicious cycle, and I'm getting tired of it.

My dad turns and walks out of the small space. The logo on the back of his cut says it all. *Sinister Sons MC.* That's what we are. Who we are. Well, what my family is. Me, not so much. My dad is the vice president of the club and overlooks all the outside sources of income, such as the garage, laundromats, and storage units. This means he watches over me because I do the books for two of those. Daily. Sometimes hourly.

I love him, I do, but ever since my mother died, he's been almost impossible. Sadly, my brothers are worse.

Six years ago, when I was sixteen, my mother passed away from an aneurism. It was a total sudden shock. She was my best friend. I know that's probably weird and all, but she was. We could talk about anything together, and she always had the best advice. She even schooled me in the art of dealing with a big house of bikers.

It's a different lifestyle we live in. My place here is to listen and do as I'm told. Not in a way that belittles me, but in a way that I respect the men in my life and their positions. Outsiders don't understand. My mother did, though, and she taught me all she knew. Only, she's gone now, and sometimes, it's really hard to bite my tongue. When you work with family, lines get crossed more often than not.

Life without my mother hasn't been easy, but we push through. Her spirit is everywhere, and that's what I hold on to. Me and my brothers, we'll get through. Somehow, we always do. Each day the void is still there, but we keep pushing.

Pulling out my round lip balm, I smear it on my lips. A man must've created this just wanting to see a bunch of women put their lips around something. Every time I apply it, it looks like I'm giving head. A chuckle escapes me as I twist the cap on and toss it into the desk drawer.

The damn books on the desk mock me. I'm going to let my brothers hear it. How damn hard is it to bring me a receipt?

Three hours later, my music is turned up and I'm on my last bit. After getting off the phone with two banks, it's finally straight. I just have to crunch a couple more numbers, and then I'm golden.

"What the fuck is this shit?" my youngest brother, Hunter, stalks into my office, snags my phone off the speaker dock, and turns off the music.

"I was listening to that." I make a grab for my phone and snatch it back, only because his hands are full of papers. Most of the time, he's quicker and just has to hold it over his head since he's tall.

"That's shit music." He's always thought my music choice is stupid, but I don't care. If I want to listen to pop, rock, and rap, so be it. Whatever mood hits me is what I listen to. Hell, my tastes change moment to moment.

Huffing out a breath, I ask, "What do you need?"

The stack of papers he has in his hand comes fluttering down on my desk, scattering all over the books and my notes like leaves falling from the trees; some even falling to the floor.

"What the fuck?" As I rise from my chair, I notice they are receipts, and while I'm happy he gave me the damn things, he just tossed them on top of everything, making another mess that I have to clean up.

I lose my temper and my tone, but a woman can only take so much.

"Watch yourself, Bristyl the pistol. Noogie time."

Jetting my hand out on my hip and cocking my foot, I call this the brother-kiss-my-ass stance. "Hunter, don't you dare."

"Oh, I dare." He makes a move to come around the desk, but I don't move. If he's going to act like a goofball, it's best to just let him do it and get over with.

He wraps his arm around my shoulder, pulling me to him and not rubbing the hell out of my hair.

"What's wrong? I know we fucked up the receipts, but you've been acting weird."

An audible sigh leaves my lips. No way I'm talking to him or anyone about this shit. Instantly, though, I calm and feel bad for my attitude, wishing they would listen to me so my job would be easier.

"Period."

His arm leaves my body like a snake is about to bite him, and he jumps back. It's funny, so I laugh. One thing is for certain, living with men has taught me that one mention of the time of the month has them backing the hell off. Hunter even brought me chocolates one time, and truthfully, I was just feeling off. It had nothing to do with the cramps. Now, it's just everything—

"You keep that shit to yourself," he barks, moving to grip the back of the chair in front of my desk.

All three of my brothers are in Sinister Sons. The Sinisters are based out of Crest, Florida, where we all grew up. As soon as my brothers could, they prospected and joined the club. All the while, I sat back and watched, happy for them, on the outside looking in. Always on the outside looking in when it comes to the Sinister Sons. My parents even kept me away from the club most of the time, only allowing me to come to specific events.

The clubhouse is an old warehouse that the Sinisters turned into their own. It has bedrooms, bathrooms, and a huge kitchen. My mother would cook for the guys, and I would try to help, even though I burned pretty much everything. Most of the time, she'd just have me sit in the kitchen and talk to her.

Down from the clubhouse is the garage. It's more of a hobby garage, but the guys use it to work on their bikes and cars. They don't take many outsiders, but my brothers do fix my car. My office is inside this building, with the door normally open. I don't hear much, because I keep to myself.

"Can you please, *please* make sure you give me these little pieces of

paper"—I pick some of them up and shake them in front of me—
"when you write a check? I can't do my job if you don't do yours."

"I'll work on it."

Hunter loves being the life of the party and spreading his jokes
around to everyone. He's tall, a gene everyone in my family seems to
have gotten, and his light brown hair is down to his chin. He shares
my blue eyes that we got from our mother. Unlike him, I also got my
mother's blonde hair. I know the women find him hot because I heard
the talk, but ewie. That shit's just weird.

"Do you need anything else? I now have a shitload to file. Thanks
for that." I plop into the seat, and it makes a squeal as the air flows out
of it. The damn thing is older than me, but this chair is history and
reminds me of my mom.

He pulls out his cigarettes and puts a tip in his mouth. "Nope, got
shit to do." As he walks from the room, I hear the click and know it's
his Zippo. He's had that thing since before he started smoking. Part of
me wonders if he took up the habit because of it, but I dismiss that
thought, knowing everyone around here smokes something. If it's not
smokes, it's weed. To each their own. Personally, I choose neither.

After filing, organizing, taking calls from people who want to rent
a unit and calls about machines taking people's money, I close down
for the day. It's early, but I did everything I need to do.

One thing I do love about my job is that as long as shit gets done,
I can come and go as I please, which means the alarm can go off a little
later than normal tomorrow.

I fill my bag as a knock comes to the door. Sterling stands there,
proud and tall, wearing a smile on his handsome face. He is my oldest
brother, Stone's, best friend from school. He joined Sinisters with my
brother and has had an eye on me for a long time. I'm not trying to be
cocky; it's a fact. One that no one here misses.

He's hot, with that scruff of dark brown hair on his face and his
short cut on top. His eyes are a deep brown that change just a bit in
the light. Women here flock to him. A lot of them. All the time.
Everywhere. This is not jealousy talking. It's a fact. You have a large
group of men around, there are bound to be women who will spread
their legs. Sterling has plenty of them, and therefore, doesn't need me.
I sure as hell don't need him.

Honestly, it's just the thought of having me with him. He doesn't
want me for the long haul, just for a quick roll in bed. That doesn't fly

with me. I know the life, and for some women, that is an arrangement they want. Good for them, but it's not for me. Bigger hopes await.

A woman can dream, right?

"Hey, Sterling. I'm just heading out. What can I do for ya?"

He swaggers in. "I'll show ya what you can do for me." His brows wiggle suggestively as his lips tip up in a sinful smirk.

I'm not one of those women who's had a crush on their brother's best friend for years and wants to fall madly in love with them and have their babies. He may think that, but he would be dead wrong. He's never been on my radar as far as men go, even when he wasn't giving it to everyone he could and then some.

"I've gotta get going." I swing my oversized bag over my shoulder and look to make sure everything is turned off.

"Let me take you out."

Here we go again.

"No." The response is immediate, as it is every other time.

"Come on. What's it take to get a man in there?" He almost groans at his words.

While rolling my eyes would be totally immature, it takes all my power not to. He's not getting *in* anywhere.

"Not interested, Sterling, you know this."

He looks me dead in the eye with a smile on his face, but it's the eyes that catch my attention. Something unrecognizable is behind them. "You know I'll treat you right."

"Back the fuck off before I stab you in the eye with a screwdriver." My middle brother, Racer, comes into the room. Damn, today has been like a revolving door. I'm so ready to go home and put an end to it.

Sterling turns toward my brother with his arms out and that same twinkle in his eye. "A man can dream."

"You fuckin' touch a hair on her head, you answer to me." Racer gets up in Sterling's face.

Racer is a bit of a hot head. Oh, who am I kidding? He's a full-out hot head. His temper can go from calm and cool to off the charts if someone fucks with him or someone he cares about. He normally has great control over it, but once it explodes … hell hath no fury.

I move to my brother and pat his chest. "I'm just leaving. Come walk me out?"

My brother doesn't move as I walk past him. Then, when I'm out of earshot, I hear, "Don't touch her unless she wants it."

Well, that's not going to happen. One thing I don't want in my life is to be with a man who can't make me his own. A man who will go off and screw other women while with me, then come back to me as if nothing happened. Sterling can't give me that. There is no trust there whatsoever.

I make my way through the stone-blocked building, feeling a slight breeze from the ventilation system as I make my way outside.

The Florida sun penetrates as the humidity instantly puts a sheen on my skin. With it being late September, it's nowhere near as bad as the summers can be. Living here, we get used to it.

I slip on my shades and see the president of the Sinister Sons, Wolf, talking to some of the brothers. He turns his head toward me, his glasses hiding whatever is on his face. Technically, he's my boss, so I'm cordial to him, giving him a slight wave. I've known him for years, though he hasn't always been president. That didn't come about until a few years ago. I can't really remember a time when I had a full-on conversation with him since my father is my go-to guy for the businesses. My father says he has an iron fist. Luckily for me, I deal with my father.

After my hand wave, I call it a day.

CHAPTER FOUR
Cooper

Music pumps through the speakers in the open room of the clubhouse. Dark paneling encases the entire room, giving it a darker feel. One wall is full of pictures, some from when I was a kid. On another wall is a bar with mirrors behind it and brightly lit signs. The bar is an L-shape and has more dents and scratches in it than a car at an impound. Each one of those marks is a memory of the life here in the Ravage MC. It will never be sanded or re-stained, not ever.

Women shake their asses on the makeshift dance floor while others mingle. It's an average Saturday night in Sumner, Georgia at the Ravage MC clubhouse. Tonight's pretty laid back, just the way I like it.

"You've got to be shittin' me," Green grunts out, tossing his cards down on the table. Gin Rummy is our game of choice and dollar bills are what's up for grabs. Green still hasn't mastered the game yet and tends to lose at every turn. It's the only way he's going to learn, though. If that happens to fatten our wallets, so be it.

"Your hand sucks." I look down to the cards and let out a chuckle. He has a three, five, seven, eight, ten, queen, and ace; suits all over the place. Possibly the worst hand ever. That shit's seriously bad, and Jacks knocked, so that means game's over.

Jacks joined the club with Green, whose real name is Ty, but got the road name Green because, when he first prospected, he was

23

beyond green when it came to club life. They were my best friends in high school and didn't have to join, but chose to. I'm happy about that. They have had my back through some tricky shit, and I trust them with my life. Even before we were technically brothers, they were there, which shows a man's character.

Playing Gin, though, Green sucks.

"Take it like a man," Jacks calls out, pulling all the money his way.

I inhale my smoke, then blow it out. "Does he know how to do that?"

Green pushes my arm. "Shut the fuck up. I need to find some pussy."

"There's enough to go around," I tell him.

"Newbie redhead over in the corner, Coop," Green says, turning back around to me. "Watchin' you like a hawk."

"When she get here?" Jacks asks, and I have the same question. She wasn't here yesterday.

"Today. Derek brought her in and got it checked with Pops. Don't know her story. Don't care," Green says, and that's enough of an answer for me.

I tilt my body so I can get a good view. She's not bad. Her hair is cut super short, while I prefer long so I have something to grab. She has very nice long legs, and her shirt pretty much shows me her plump breasts. *What the hell; I'm bored, anyway.*

"Let me go see if the carpet matches the drapes," I say, rising from my seat.

"That's overused, brother," Jacks tells me, and I shrug, not giving a shit.

Crooking my finger at the woman, she comes over immediately.

An hour later, I find out that they do match.

"About fuckin' time. Where the hell were you?" Ryker asks as I enter the large out-building we built three years ago. Pops said we needed more room and a place that was locked up tight, so he built this. There are no windows and only two doors. It's reinforced steel walls with cameras everywhere on the outside and alarms for any unwelcome guests. We don't need anyone seeing what goes on behind them. Not that we've had any problems.

"Watchin' Austyn and Nox." I rub my hand over my exhausted face.

I love my siblings, but fuck, they're a damn handful. They fight all the damn time about stupid shit they don't even care about in ten minutes. Being so much older, it's different having them so young, but it's my family.

"Get over here and help." Ryker loads up a padded, wooden crate, screwing the top of it shut with an electric screw gun, the sound buzzing off the walls.

"This shit isn't gonna pack itself," Green says as I get to work.

Guns. They are always on the market. The bigger, the better, and the more money earned. I learned to put together and take apart just about every type of gun there is doing this job. Ravage makes most of our money from the guns. With laws changing and more people wanting to protect what's theirs, more guns are in demand.

"You ready for the rally? Rhys says we're pullin' out on Thursday."

"Hell yeah." Every year, we head down to Florida for Burnout Beach. It's a smaller rally, not like Sturgis; more low key. This one is more for making connections with other clubs. There are bands, beer, and broads. Lots of all three. While we do accomplish business normally, there's a lot of time to let loose.

We normally go a few days early to do the actual business, then it's time to have fun.

The door swings open, with Rhys and Buzz entering the building.

"How's it goin'?" Green calls out as they step forward.

As a kid, I was terrified of Rhys. His demeanor does not invite outsiders whatsoever. Now that I'm an adult, I'm just happy he's on my side. Even having two little girls hasn't cracked his armor. Although, I did see him watch some princess movie a while back, but I never said anything. Personally, I think he's gotten harder, especially with his kids. They don't move or sneeze without him or his woman, Tanner, knowing about it. He takes protective to an entirely different level.

Buzz is a tech genius and has been with the club for well over twenty years. He taught me how to hack, best places for cameras when doing surveillance, and how to dissect a hard drive to get information. He says he's not getting any younger and needs to pass on his skills. He has two twin boys, Raiden and Axton. They're only nine, but I'm sure Buzz has already begun teaching them what he knows. That could be disaster, because the man could hack classified shit. Hopefully his kids don't cause too much chaos.

Buzz has a twin brother, Breaker, but his kids are still pretty little.

"Princess is askin' for some help down at X. Anyone want the job?" Buzz asks on a chuckle.

Studio X is a strip club that Ravage owns and my mother runs. Tug's ol' lady, Blaze, used to dance there, but now she does the books. There's tons of history between them, but it's theirs to tell.

"Fuck yeah," Green and Jacks say in unison.

"I'm down," Ryker adds.

"Sure. I'm always down to see some tits and ass."

X is a smorgasbord of anything a man could want or need. Blonde, brunette, redheads. Hell, we have one that has purple hair. You name it, X has it.

Working at X is a huge perk of our job. One that we take advantage of regularly. When I was a teen, I'd bust a nut to go to X. Now, coming and going is a wonderful pleasure.

"Boys," Rhys says as we begin to walk out after packaging our last gun. "Try not to fuck them all. It only leads to bad shit."

"We'll try," Ryker says, waving his hand in the air. I'm ready for the show.

CHAPTER FIVE

Bristyl

The red polish sparkles on my toes as I finish my forced pedicure. Toes, feet in particular, are a thing with me. Women, men—it doesn't matter. They have shitty looking feet, it grosses me out. It's not like feet attacked me at some point in my life or anything. It's just my thing, and why my little toes are pristine.

Leah, my best friend from high school, plops down on the bed, making me jump.

"You're damn lucky I already closed the bottle." The damage done by nail polish on my purple and black bedspread would be a mess. One I don't feel like cleaning up or having to buy a new one.

"Whatever," she grumbles with a smile. "So, is your dad going to let you go to the rally?"

Leah has been around for the past five years, and she's stuck around because I can trust her. Between girls wanting to be my friend to have a shot at my brothers or the guys thinking I'm an easy lay, I lost a lot of faith in people. My dad always says, *You only trust your family.* I consider Leah my family.

Over the years, she's had my back on more than one occasion. The best part, she never asks about my brothers or about going to the club.

She's my friend and wants nothing in return, other than friendship back.

"He'll probably give me shit about it." More than shit, actually. Even being twenty-one-years-old, my father treats me as if I'm sixteen. I love him, but it's getting suffocating. There have been times on and off when I've had to be locked down at home because he said he had to keep me safe. I know it involves the club, but long ago, I learned not to ask questions. Club business isn't my business.

I have my own place. Well, partially. The small house is right off the main house where I grew up and where my father lives. I have privacy, but I'm shrouded by my father's protection. I know he's being careful, but the older I get, the more it weighs on me like lead—that urge to be free and be my own person, not shielded and confined.

"We have to go. It'll be so much fun."

Leah went with me last year to Burnout Beach, and we did have fun. My brothers only found us a couple of times and scared two guys away, which was annoying. My father didn't like it one bit. He had two prospects follow us from a distance, but they kept their cool and didn't intervene much. The fight about having those two men follow me wasn't pretty, but I had no choice except to suck it up.

These rallies are … crazy. I'm not even sure if that's the right word for them. Lots of bikers from all over the country, but mostly southern states, come to Florida for it. It's built on the premise that they all get together to connect. At least, that's what my brothers told me. My perspective is that it's so they can get drunk and screw.

What I love about them is the bands and dancing. I could spend the entire time just watching the different bands perform. This year, one of my favorites, Demon's Wings, is going to be there. My plan is to enjoy their music to the fullest. If I happen to stare at Shane Stevenson with his blue-gray eyes and short, dark hair the entire time, so be it.

I'm not going to lie. There's some great eye candy there as well. The women … I could go without seeing all the tits and ass flying around. But it is what it is.

"I'll make it work." I haven't said a word about the rally to any of my family. My brothers have talked about, but I keep my mouth shut. I do this for one reason and one reason only: if my father doesn't think I'm going, he can't have guys watching the entire time. So, I will wait until he's gone then head out.

Sneaky, yes. It's easier that way. He doesn't have to be the bad guy, and I don't have to get pissed off at him. Win-win.

Leah eyes me, smiles, grabs my laptop, and fires it up.

I chuckle, falling back on the pillows, a puff of air exploding around me. "Let's see what today brings."

"This is funny shit. We couldn't make it up if we tried."

About six months ago, Leah signed up for an internet dating website. She had high hopes of meeting someone, but instead, she gets propositioned with some crazy stuff.

"Alright. What has love chosen for you today?"

"Oh shit, there's like, seven messages."

I stare up at the ceiling, her clicking of the keys the only sound in the room. "You're hot, what do you expect?"

She is. Long, dark hair, a kickass body, and stunning brown eyes. Why she wants to look for love on a dating site is beyond me. To each their own. I'm here for moral support and the laughs.

"Oh, my God!" Her hand flies over her mouth, and I sit up instantly, looking at the screen.

An image stares back at me. It takes me a moment to digest it. A woman is lying on her back, legs up, knees on either side of her face, ass in the air. A man is sitting on top of her, legs spread while reading the paper, both naked. It looks like he's taking a shit on her.

"What the hell is this?"

"Apparently, this is the 'butter churner.' It's a sexual position this guy wants to do to me."

I burst out laughing, unable to hold it in. It racks my body so hard that I shake uncontrollably. "What! He wants to shit on you and read the paper?"

She scrolls down through his message. "He says he likes having his women sit like this. His dick inside her, while he sits and either reads the paper or watches television."

"Like a damn chair? Don't they make some kind of blowup doll or something for that?"

"Hell if I know. Wouldn't it, like, break a guy's dick to just sit in that position? I mean, he'd have to, like, push his dick, like, straight down. How is that even comfortable?"

Laughter bubbles in the room, bouncing off the walls and echoing back. Tears stream from my eyes, and my stomach clenches.

"How does this relate to a butter churner? Where would that name even come from?"

Leah hiccups her laugh. "I don't know. Maybe he likes to circle his hips or move up and down. Oh, my God, this is just nuts."

"So, he's out."

"Ya think?"

I fall back on the bed. "What else did ya get?"

She clicks around. "A marriage proposal and five date requests. Oh, Lord …"

"What now?"

She brings the laptop over to me and sets it on my belly. I read: *I want you to whip me and spank me. Make me drink your piss. I'm your slave; you're my master.* This guy didn't send a picture, thank goodness, but his profile picture is so fake.

"Leah, that guy is a model. I've seen him in magazines. There's no way this is legit. Someone is yanking your chain."

She lies down beside me and looks at the picture. "No way."

"Lord, the things we do for entertainment. You're not going on any of those."

"I know. It sucks. Where are the good men?"

"Damned if I know."

Bang … Bang.

My eyes flutter open at the sound. I look around, noting I'm in my small living room, lying on the couch. I must've fallen asleep. Naps are my friend, not that I get a lot of them.

"Bristyl! Open up," Stone's voice comes through the door.

Rolling off the couch with a groan, I move toward the door and open it.

My brother breezes right in, almost knocking me over in the process. *Come on in.*

He enters the kitchen and opens my refrigerator, his head buried inside of it.

"Sure, Stone, eat whatever you'd like. Drink whatever you'd like."

"Shut it," he says back, pulling out a small bit of a sandwich I didn't eat a few days ago and chomping on it.

A smile plays on my lips, remembering I should have thrown it away because I dropped the sandwich on the ground. Serves him right.

"You bellowed?" I ask, resting my hip on the side counter.

My kitchen is small. It has the necessities—fridge, stove, sink, and microwave—but it's about the size of a postage stamp. My father redid the countertops and put in new cabinets about three years ago, and I've kept it in really good shape. My cooking skill suck, so it's golden for me.

"We got a run. We'll be gone for a few days," he tells me.

I shrug. "And?" This isn't something new. My father and several of the guys go out on runs all the time. I don't know what they do on them, and I don't want to know. As long as they come home in one piece, that's all I give a shit about.

"Most of us are going, including Hunter, Racer, Dad and me."

This does come as a bit of a shock. Usually, one or two of my brothers stay behind. Someone is always at the clubhouse or garage when I'm there for work. It's a bit unusual, but it's their club and how they run it. I can't say it doesn't give me a twinge of anxiety, though, and I'm not sure why. The air in the club has been different these past few weeks, and I wish I knew the reason. It must just be me.

"Okay …?" I draw out, waiting for more of this puzzle to come together.

He shoves the sandwich into his mouth, then grabs a soda I didn't see him pull out, popping the top and taking a swig. He's tall, go figure. Unlike the rest of us, Stone has dark hair, almost black. He wears it long on the top and shaved on the sides. He has a slight beard and hazel eyes. They aren't blue or green, but both. When I was younger, I used to hope I could have his eyes. Then reality kicked in.

"You're on storage and laundromat duty."

"Stone, I got this. I do it every day."

"But one of us goes and fixes whatever's wrong. You either need to call in one of our people or take a prospect with you if something happens."

"Got it."

No way in hell I'm calling a prospect to go with me to fix something. Normal things that happen are the bill validator jams up or someone can't get a machine to work. It's nothing I can't handle. Yes, it's nice to call one of my brothers and have them do it, but I'm more than capable. Needing a babysitter is not on my agenda.

"Just try not to burn it down."

I hit him on his shoulder. "I only burned a trailer, and it wasn't my fault!" I charge back with a smile in my tone. "That old thing needed to go, anyway."

"Bristyl, you can't burn a man's camper on storage unit property. At least take it out in the back field."

"I didn't mean to." I really didn't. Its propane tank had a leak, and I didn't know.

I had just tried starting to smoke. I lit a cigarette and *boom*. Luckily, I wasn't hurt. Thrown back and hit my head, but not hurt. That was also the last smoke I put between my lips.

"Mean to or not, no fires."

"No fires," I repeat. "I got this, Stone. You don't need to worry."

He steps closer and wraps his arm around me before pulling me to him. I inhale the leather, smoke, and spice that is my brother. The scent is a comfort. His lips touch the top of my head, adding to that warm feeling.

"I'll always worry about you ... until I take my fuckin' dying breath."

I squeeze him a little bit harder. "I know, but you gotta let me loose a bit."

"Never." He gives me another kiss then steps back. "Alright, you need anything, you can call us. We won't be able to come back, though. We'll be home in two days."

"Yes, kemosabe."

"Smartass," he grumbles, going toward the door. Gotta love my brother. "And, Bristyl, stay aware," he warns before stepping through and taking off.

The warning isn't unusual, but the way he said it is. Stay aware seems like there's an actual threat, but no one has said anything.

It must be in my head.

CHAPTER SIX
Cooper

The wind in my hair and heat on my skin is freeing. It's life. Being on a bike, not surrounded by metal, is like floating on air. The high from riding is something I hope never dies. Riding with my club, my family, it's unexplainable. A brother flanking me to the front, the side, and the rear, we move as if we are one. And we are. There isn't a thing I wouldn't do for any of these men, and them for me.

We've been riding for the past four hours with a few stops along the way. Now we are almost at our first destination—a meeting with a client who wants us to transport for him.

Normally, Ravage is up for anything, but this time, it's coke. We don't deal in coke. Never have. That shit is fierce. Weed, we're good with. But since most states have legalized it and people can grow the shit in their basement, that leaves little to transport. We kept to guns because they are lucrative and in demand.

Coke is in demand, too, but something we just haven't done. The guy, Tommy Bean, wants a sit down, and we voted to do it at church. Pops thought it would be good to keep relations because we do supply Tommy with guns. Rhys has some issues, not giving a flying fuck about biker relations. He says he's not a fucking PR person.

He's right, but times are changing. Our word is and always has been our bond. Now we've expanded so much that we need to keep everyone on point. Knowledge is power, and we need to know exactly

33

what Tommy wants to do with his product and where he wants it to go. The main goal in this meeting is to get information and smooth shit over when we decline.

While I'm all for keeping everyone on an even keel, I'm there with Rhys. If they come at us and don't back down, we'll do what we have to do to extinguish it.

I'm not dealing with anyone trying to get us to do anything. We are Ravage—we do what we want, when we want. If we have to take out the whole crew, so be it. It'll be in Tommy's best interest to remember that.

Pops leads the pack, with Becs, Dagger, GT, Rhys, my father, Tug, Breaker, and Buzz right behind him. Dagger has been with the club since my great-grandfather Striker was around. He's a burly man with long hair he braids down his back and always has a red, white, and blue bandana around his head. The stories of him back in the day paint him as a man who played with a lot of pussy. Now, his ol' lady, Mearna, would gut him, and he knows it.

Tug is another brother who joined back when Buzz and Breaker did. His ol' lady, Blaze, used to strip at X, but now works side by side with my mother.

After them are Green, Ryker, Derek, Jacks, and myself.

We are one. Pops turns his bike, we all do. We are a pack. A family. We follow each move Pops makes, keeping our eyes open to everything around us. Observation is key, and knowing our surroundings at all times is a must.

Back in the day, we'd have someone staying back at the clubhouse to take care of the women and children. Now, Ravage doesn't have any threats or reason for such protection. That doesn't mean we left them alone. Four prospects are at the clubhouse, just in case.

We follow Pops into the parking lot of a place called Schooners Bar, off the main highway. I take note of the five bikes in the parking lot, three trucks, and two cars. There's wide open space around the blue tinted block building; therefore, no surprises.

Tug and Buzz break off, and Ryker follows them. They're going around the building to make sure it's secure. We may not have a threat, but we take our safety very seriously.

Surprisingly, none of the ol' ladies wanted to come with us on this trip. It shocked me because my mother is always up for an adventure, but she said she had shit to deal with at X.

Pops parks his bike, and we follow suit, making a row of steel machines in front of the bar. I reach around my back and make sure my gun is holstered. Even with conceal and carry, it's not smart for a man with a cut on his back to be found with a gun, but I refuse to be without. The metal has been checked and is totally clean, just in case.

"Let's do this. Florida is calling," Pops says after Rhys gives him the all-clear, strolling into the place. He's as confident as ever, but the small twitch in his cheek is leading me more to my conclusion that he's about done.

The inside is dark, so I remove my shades to see clearly. It's a typical dive bar that looks like it should have been shut down years ago, but somehow, they keep it afloat. There's a large bar to the left, and a wide-open space to the right. There are two doors. One has a window and looks like it leads to the kitchen area. The other door, I assume, is a bathroom. I've learned never to assume. Find out facts. Facts, you can deal with. Assumptions, you can't.

Tommy sits in the corner of the bar. His hair has a comb-over that looks like it's been fucking teased by a brush. It seems he's having a hard time with getting older and losing his hair. Three other men sit around him. Sizing them up, they have bulk, but numbers alone have us on top.

"Tommy," Pops greets, strolling up to the table.

Tommy rises and holds out his hand. "Pops and the Ravage boys."

His other men stand, and we all shake.

"Nice of ya ta stop by," Tommy says.

With the vehicles in the lot, I clock there are ten, maybe more, if they had passengers. A lone bartender is behind the bar so that would be five people. Two older men sit at poker machines, slipping coins into the slot. That's seven. There are at least three more.

I grab my father's attention and angle my head to the left.

"Just gonna check things out," Pops says when Tommy looks over at me as I move to the kitchen door.

"What, don't trust me?" he says on a laugh.

"Only men I trust are the ones at my back," Pops replies as I make my way to the door with the window.

Peering in, I see one older male with a pot belly stirring something in a pot. That leaves two guys unaccounted for.

Entering the space, the older man's head pops up. "Can I help you?"

"Who else is back here with you?"

"Who the fuck are you?" he retorts.

Not wanting to pull my gun out just yet, I say, "I'm just checkin' shit out. Need to know if anyone's back here with you."

"And I don't give a fuck."

Having enough of the man's shit—hell, I gave him more chances than most of the guys would—I pull out my gun and point it at him. "See this, motherfucker? Tell me who's back here with you."

He drops the ladle into the pot and puts his hands up in the air. "Now, now, calm down."

"Don't fuckin' tell me what I don't want to hear. Answer the damn question."

"Brother?" I hear Ryker behind me as he steps into the room. "Everything okay in here?"

"We've got at least two people unaccounted for, judging from the vehicles outside. Trying to get Boiler Bob here to tell me if there's anyone back here, but I guess we're gonna have to check the coolers."

"You don't need to do that," Boiler Bob says, looking at the deep freezer that could totally have a person inside of it. What the ever-loving fuck?

Ryker steps toward the freezer while I keep my eye on the guy. Gun extended, he opens the freezer.

I glance at him.

"Nothing."

"There's nobody in here. Don't know why you've come in here with all the metal. If you saw an old black four-by-four, that's Willard's. His wife had to come get his drunk-ass and take him home. There's no one back here."

"Why the fuck couldn't you have just said that, asshole?"

Ryker pulls out some cheese and starts eating it. He shrugs. "I'm fuckin' hungry."

"There's one left." The gun is aimed directly at Boiler Bob's head.

"That's probably Sally's car. A beat-up Honda Civic? It breaks down all the damn time, I swear. She uses this place for storage. She's one of the waitresses on the weekend," he responds.

Thinking back to the cars, he's right. One of them was a piece of shit Civic that needs serious help.

"Thanks."

Entering the main room, Ryker goes to check the bathroom,

finding no one.

Pops and Tommy are in discussions with Becs, GT, Rhys, Dagger, and Tug, sitting in chairs, while everyone else is either behind them or at the bar.

Me, I order a damn beer and breathe for a moment, keeping my ear on the conversation as I sit next to Ryker, who seems to be doing the same thing. Being in the know is a must in this business.

"Nah, Tommy, we're not runnin'. You need your supply from us, you give us a call and we'll get what you need," Pops says calmly, but there's tension in his voice, one that I've only heard a few times in the last couple of months.

The worry hits me like a weight in my gut. It's getting closer to time.

"It's only a few runs. Five tops to get it where it needs to be," Tommy tries, his guys looking back and forth between him and Pops.

"Told ya no, and I don't say what I don't mean."

The air becomes thick with tension.

Abandoning my beer, both Ryker and I move to stand behind Pops with our brothers. If something is going to happen, we're prepared. Always prepared.

"We were really hopin' to come to an agreement here," Tommy says, scratching his cheek.

My eyes burn into the surroundings, checking every single person. Tommy's little gesture could be a signal for a gun raid, bomb explosion—hell, just about anything at this point.

There's nothing out of order.

"You want to talk our supply, we can talk. Other than that, Tommy, Ravage has lines. That one, we don't cross."

"Since when? I remember a time when Ravage did anything and everything," Tommy fires back.

"Don't need to give you any explanation. The answer is no. You gonna let this rest, or we gonna take care of this shit right here and now?"

Tommy's eyes come to each one of us who are supporting and standing by our president with everything we got. No way in hell those three will make it out of here alive. It'll be a bitch to clean up with the innocents around, but we'll make it work.

Pops clears his throat obviously having enough of his time wasted.

When Tommy's focus goes back to Pops, he sighs deeply. "Fine, no mess. I'll find someone else, but you gotta know ..." Tommy leans forward on his forearms. "You bastards are some of the best to transport this shit. You'd make a fuckin' killing."

Pops holds his hand out. "We have a deal. Not another word about your dust. You need us, call."

Tommy reluctantly holds out his hand and shakes Pops'. "Not gonna fuck up a good thing with Ravage, Pops. Honorable man. Thanks for takin' the time to come see me."

Pops nods, releasing Tommy's hand before standing. "We gotta roll."

And that's what we do. Roll the hell out of bumfuck nowhere and head to the booze, babes, and beaches.

Sunny Florida. The sunshine state, or some other bullshit like that. We've been here for three days. Pops has had meetings in his hotel room off and on, while me and some of the guys went to the beach for a bit. Nothing like seeing beautiful women in bikinis.

It's been pretty low key, but everyone is starting to show up for Burnout Beach tomorrow.

"What the hell?" Ryker jumps back as water sloshes out of the washing machine and onto the floor in pools. The water doesn't stop, either, even when the water from the wash is out. No, it keeps pouring and pouring like the damn Niagara Falls.

"Where's the shutoff?" I ask, moving toward the machine and reaching behind it. I can't see the damn shutoffs since they're behind some fancy-ass board thing, proving to be no help at all. I pound hard on the wood and hear it crunch, but it doesn't break.

"Here, let me try. You've got monster hands," Green says as I step away, my pants and boots now soaked.

I look around for an attendant, but there is none. There is a number, though, so I pull out my phone and dial it.

It goes to voicemail.

I call it again. Same thing.

I call it again.

"Laundry Services," a woman's voice comes over the line in almost a purr. Not one like some of the girls at the club use to get us in bed. No, this woman has more of a natural purr that's low, yet not a growl. It's sexy as all hell.

"I'm at your laundromat, and there's water everywhere. We're trying to get to the shutoffs, but they're covered."

"Shit. I'm on my way." That voice. Damn. She doesn't even let me enjoy it before she hangs up.

I toss my phone on my bag sitting on the table; no need for it to get wet, too.

The water slows to a trickle as Green pops up from the back.

"Those fuckers have rust on them." He wipes his hand on his jeans, leaving an orange mark behind. "Fuck, now I gotta wash these."

"Look at me, dickhead." Ryker holds his arms out, standing in a puddle of water, wet from pretty much the chest down. His clothes are scattered on the floor in a soppy mess. "My boots are gonna take forever to dry. Fuck!" he growls.

"Calm your shit."

The other customers in the place are staring at us, but not one came over to help the situation. Figures.

"We don't need a stir." We never need the cops in our business, and Ryker screaming and carrying on will definitely get one called. I don't feel like calling my dad or Pops and asking them to bail my ass out of jail for fucking water.

"Sonofabitch," he growls low, picking up his clothes and tossing them into another machine. "This one had better fuckin' work." He jams the coins into it, and it begins its cycle. The water on the floor is steadily flowing into the drain, but it's still wet as hell.

"I'm gonna change." Ryker grabs his duffle and heads toward the bathroom. It's funny seeing him razzed because it rarely happens. Ryker is always a joke a minute or a smooth line.

The simple joys in life we have to suck up.

I switch over my clothes and toss them into a dryer. Green does the same. Jacks said he didn't need to come. No doubt he's asleep. That man loves his sleep. Can't blame him. I like mine, too ... sometimes.

"What's going on?" the purred voice says from the door.

I turn. Standing in the doorway is a woman in very well-worn jeans and a black T-shirt that stretches across her ample chest, the V showing just a touch of it. Her blonde hair is long, silky, yet wavy at the bottom. There's no black roots, so that shit is real. Her light, crystal blue eyes come to me, pause on a stutter for a moment, and then her gaze goes to the floor, seeing the huge puddle of mess.

"Shit." She pulls out her phone and makes a call. "Need you here ten minutes ago." She pushes her phone in the back pocket of her jeans, sliding it down the curve of her ass.

"Who called?" she questions, looking around to each one of us.

I step up. "Me."

Her eyes travel my body, and then she clears her throat. "Sorry about this. Sometimes the seals come loose. I've been after my plumber to redo the shutoffs so they're easier to get to." She reaches in her front pocket and pulls out two twenties. "Here, these washes and dries are on me with our apologies."

Ryker takes that moment to come up and pluck the money out of my hand. "Thank you spanky much," he says on a chuckle.

The woman bustles past everyone, ignoring Ryker, and heads to a door in the back, inserting a key then stepping inside. When she comes out, she has a mop bucket and a mop. She's put her hair back in one of those messy bun things on her head that my sister wears all the time. With it out of her face, she's even more striking, wiping any comparison to my sister out of the park.

What the hell is wrong with me?

Green chuckles. "See somethin' you like?"

"Shut the fuck up."

He laughs harder.

"I know I do," Ryker says, taking a few steps toward her. "Hey, honey, I'm Ryker. And you are ...?"

"Busy," she replies, pulling the mop out and beginning to clean up the mess.

"Burn!" Green calls out, and Ryker laughs.

"Let me help you. Then we can get to know each other," Ryker tells her.

I feel my blood begin to boil. I'm not sure why. There's no reason for its cause, but it's happening.

The woman looks down at Ryker, and then bursts out laughing. It's like her voice, a purr-ish laugh that has my dick turning to granite.

I follow her gaze and a laugh escapes me, too. On Ryker's feet are Snoopy Christmas socks.

"What the fuck, brother?" I ask, not bothering to hide my amusement.

"My sister got them for me. Shut the hell up."

"And you decided to wear them to Florida? Nice, Ryker," Green chides.

"Normally no one sees the damn things," he grumbles.

The woman sucks in a breath, smiles, and swishes the mop back and forth.

"Next time, I'd leave those at home," Green says as Ryker sits next to him on the hard, plastic chairs along the wall where the windows line it.

"What can I say? This dog's got tricks."

"Better find new ones," Green responds.

"Sorry about that," I tell her, not a hundred percent why. Am I really sorry, or is it just an excuse to talk to her? The answer is unclear.

Her eyes meet mine, and I swear I can see myself in them for the briefest moment, before she shrugs and goes back to cleaning. "I'm used to it. No big deal."

"Used to getting hit on?"

"That's not what I meant." She stops like she's thinking about something, then continues, "I have older brothers who give me shit all the time. I get it."

"I'm Cooper," I say, not asking for her name. A small part of me wonders if she'll tell me.

"Bristyl. Now, can you step back so I can clean this shit up? My plumber is going to be here soon, and I don't need anyone falling and breaking a hip." She looks around at the older lady using the dryer at the end. Her quirky sense of humor gets to me.

I take a step backward.

"Thanks."

"Brother?" Green calls from the table.

I close my eyes and shake myself, wanting to ignore him, but then I turn toward my brothers.

"You alright?"

"Fine. Let's get this shit done."

Women are like flowers; there are so many and so many varieties out there to choose from. This woman is just one of many. I have to remember that.

So what if her voice is sin, along with her body? So what if she has a wicked tongue? None of that matters.

CHAPTER SEVEN

Bristyl

Holy hells bells.

I'm not sure if I should be pissed that my brothers and father left me to deal with this mess or thank them for the gorgeous eye candy. Not that I would, because they'd have a fit either way, but damn. Maybe it's my mom smiling down on me, giving me a ray of sunshine through this mess.

All three of the guys are hot in their own way. By the cuts on their backs, they belong to the Ravage Motorcycle Club. Here for the rally, of course, and will be gone in a flash. That's how it is. What the hell, I'll enjoy the view while I can.

I sop up the water and wring out the mop head, then repeat ... again and again.

Ryker, who boldly introduced himself, is a player. Yep, seen hundreds of them in my day growing up in the club. Tattoos, sexy vibe ... I bet he doesn't even have to ask women, just crooks his finger.

The other man, who I'm not sure his name, looks a little lighter in a way, but I'm not sure how to describe it.

Cooper, though. My heavens. Talk about charismatic, and I got that just from the few words he spoke to me. Hell, I get it just from being in the same room with him. It's like he oozes it out of his pores, releasing it out in the world for women to fall at his feet and beg. Then there's the hair. I can't call it light, and it's definitely not dark. It's a unique combination of the two; light browns intertwined with a few darker browns, giving his hair a shade I haven't seen before. Like a caramel color with an edge, and long. So much so that he has a hair tie wrapped around his wrist. No doubt he puts it up regularly. I'd put money on it only amping up his sexiness.

When our eyes connected for that brief moment, the blue popped out in his. I also noticed some navy around the edges. That combination of hair and eyes ... Be still my deprived heart.

The way his pants ride low on his hips makes me want to give up all kinds of things to get him to raise his arms above his head so his black T-shirt rises up and I can see what's underneath.

He has tattoos running all up his left arm, disappearing under his shirt. I can see some black poking through the top at his neck, too. It piques my curiosity, wanting to find out what he's hiding.

I shake my head and squeeze out the mop. It's been way too long since ... Never mind.

The front door opens and in strolls Mr. Draker. The guy is older; late sixties, early seventies. He's been our plumber for years, and a man my father trusts to take care of problems.

"What'd ya got here?" he asks, strolling in with his bag in hand.

I look at the floor then up at him. "What do you think? I had everyone take a piss all over the floor?"

Chuckles come from the corner where the three hot bikers sit and wait for their clothes to dry.

"I told you we needed new shutoffs for each machine. That was on your list four months ago, and now it's been moved to priority, as in— do it now." He jumps a bit at my tone, but doesn't balk.

This is the part of the businesses I don't like—when you hire someone to do a job, and they don't follow through. It's happening more and more. I try to handle it all because if my father or brothers did, hell hath no fury. It just makes everything so much worse.

"I was just comin' to do that today, Ms. Bristyl."

Stopping short of rolling my eyes, I say, "Yeah, and the pigs are due to shoot out of my ass at any minute. This needs to be done now. I called my cleaner on the way here. Most of it is sopped up, but you'll have to work around the customers until the place is cleared out. I don't care how you do it; just make it happen."

A loose strand of hair falls into my eyes, and I blow it up out of my way. This is business, and if he doesn't want to do his job, then I'll find someone who can. Then I'll have to explain it to my father, and he'll be pissed I didn't come to him first. One step at a time.

"I can shut off these and do the pipes, then the others. There should be no need to shut the place down."

"Timeline. When's it going to be done?" My tone is sharp. I'm seriously frustrated with this man.

"Give me a week to get it all switched over."

"If it's not done by then, I'm finding someone who can do it."

"I understand."

He better understand. Sinister Sons is huge in this town, and he knows who owns this place. One word, and that will be it.

I like handling everything on my own, though. It's an independence thing. I don't have it in my life as much as I want, but this I can control.

When clapping comes from the corner, I narrow my eyes. That is, until I see the smirk on Cooper's face. Then I turn and put the damn mop bucket away, needing to get out of here and breathe. For some reason, he has a power to suck the oxygen out of me.

Coming out of the room, Cooper and his guys are pulling clothes out of the dryers and a washer, then beginning to fold. I can't help looking. I mean, come on, my eyes just travel there on instinct.

His black briefs are sexy as all hell. I need a cold shower.

"Sorry again for the trouble," I say on a wave.

Some words are returned as I exit quickly, getting the hell out of Dodge.

"Don't be pissed at me." Whenever anyone starts a conversation off with those words, you know you're going to be pissed at the end. It's a red flag with a bull running toward it. It's a lit match about to be thrown into a fire pit doused in gasoline.

"What am I going to be pissed about?"

Leah just walked in the door. Her navy shirt is cut short, exposing her midriff, and her shorts are tight, but she's covered. One thing I love about her is she's not over the top. Some of the women at the rally dress in bikinis or fishnet with only a small piece of tape covering their nipples. I wouldn't want to get caught for indecent exposure or anything. My big hiccup is some men take the lack of clothes as a welcoming invitation, which no man should do.

Me, I'm super simple. Jean shorts that totally cover my ass, coming down an inch or two. They're not loose, but I don't have a damn camel toe or any of that crap. I went with my favorite Demon's Wings tank with a sports bra underneath it. It is Florida, after all. And if I'm going to be dancing, I need air. Tossing on my flip flops, I'm ready to go.

"Your makeup is pretty," she says to me as we exit the house and I lock it up.

I shrug. "I just went for a little bit of a smoky eye. Tell me what I'm pissed about?" We move to my Dodge Challenger SRT, get in, and I turn her over, making her purr like a kitten in heat. If Leah thinks she's going to detour me, she's sadly mistaken.

"A guy I met on that site is going to meet me there."

The urge to slam on my brakes hits me hard, along with slapping her upside her damn head. "You're just shitting me, right?" I try with a small bit of hope, knowing in my gut it's worthless. I'm pissed.

"No, his name is Nick, and he's really nice. We've been chatting on the dating site, and he said he's coming to the rally this weekend. I told him I'd text him and we could meet up."

If my grip got any tighter on the steering wheel, my strength would snap the damn thing off Hulk style.

"Is he with a club?" There have been a couple of times in my life where our family was at dinner and another club showed up wanting to talk to my father. The situation got heated when my father refused, and my brothers rose from their seats. No, my family wouldn't like it if this guy were in another club, but why else would he be at a bike rally.

She clicks her tongue, in thought. "I don't know. I didn't ask him."

"Leah, that should have been the first question. Hello, he's coming to a rally. Yes, we have non-clubbers here, but what if ...?" I let my words trail off.

What if what? I know what my father and brothers do isn't legal, but I don't know any details, which keeps me clean. What if this guy is an enemy or something? One of the ones that my brothers are always keeping me safe from? Maybe I'm just being a stick in the mud and need to live a little, but uneasiness prickles my skin.

"Relax. If it doesn't work out, we go dance. It gives me an out."

"You're nuts," I tell her.

"You love me."

"Yeah, I do."

Finding a place to park is a pain in the ass, and after hiking the mile up the hill, we finally make it to the rally.

Music from three stages blares as men and women run around, beers and cocktails in their hands. A huge sign hangs above the road, welcoming all bikers. The atmosphere is electric and pulsing with an energy you only get when coming to a testosterone-filled place like this.

Venders line up their tents with barely clothed women trying to push the latest power drink or tire brand. If you wanted to take the time to visit them all, it would take an entire day. Each one yells out at us, trying to grab our attention, but we keep on moving. No prize they have is on my list of must haves in the world.

A burly man with leather chaps stops in front of me. He's handsome in his rode-hard biker way. His beard is long, and he has a red, white, and blue bandana over his forehead with a long braid going down his back.

"How you ladies doin'?" he asks in a smooth tenor.

Another man steps around and puts his hand on bandana man's shoulder. This guy makes me want to take a step backward. He's mean-looking, hair cut to his scalp, and tattoos covering scars. He screams danger and has a don't-mess-with-me vibe I'm pretty sure I could feel from another planet.

"Mearna, brother," he says in a low voice.

"I'm talkin'."

"Yeah, and you fuckin' told me to say somethin' when you get like this. I'm sayin' it and steppin' back." The scary man does just that, hands raised as he takes a few steps backward.

Bandana man rubs his hand over his face. "Fuckin' hell. My ol' lady'll cut my dick off. As you were, ladies," he grumbles, moving out of our path.

We move quickly.

"What the hell was that?" Leah asks as we make our way toward one of the stages. I'm hoping this is the one for Demon's Wings.

"Just a big man seeing two chicks and hittin' on them. Not a big deal," I tell her, because it's not. She should be used to it after last year and getting hit on.

"I wouldn't want to be the woman who's gonna cut off that guy's dick. And did you see that other man? I think he could have broken us like twigs. They remind me a lot of your dad and his crew."

"Crew?" I question with a laugh. "That's one way to see it."

"Drinks!" she yells out, making her way to one of the many stands. Behind them are women in bikinis with little bits of tape or fabric covering their lady bits. Tip jars sit out on the bar. These women are going to make bank judging from the hungry gazes around them. The ones who dance and put on a show will do even better. They catch the attention of the men and women, so it's double the money.

We order drinks then head toward the stage, seeing a large sign that says *"Demon's Wings at seven p.m."*

"They're here!" I may have given a little excited jump, but come on, this is why I came, just to see them. Well, to see Shane, that is. The other guys are hot, don't get me wrong, but Shane, the lead singer … hot damn.

Leah looks at her phone. "I got a text. I need to meet him over at the beer tent."

Okay, that's vague. "Which beer tent? There's, like, ten of them."

"The one near the tire burn out."

At Point, a band I've never heard of, comes on and begins playing. I really want to dance, but you never leave your friend alone. Going with her is a must.

"Alright, but I'm not going to be hanging around you two if you're going to be all over each other." I may have that code, but I will drag her away before any of that shit happens. Even as beautiful as she is, she's meek on the guy side, with only a few ex-boyfriends. She may have other thoughts on it, but we shall see.

Making our way through the horde, I'm telling pretty much every single person I come in contact with sorry for bumping into them. The burn out is a hot place, and the bodies are deep on the ground level. The only way to see anything is if you go up into the bleachers, which have tons of open areas.

I pull Leah's arm, motioning for her to follow me up the metal risers. She does, her eyes all over the place, looking for this Nick guy. This is a bad idea. I feel it in my gut, and the prickles are coming back to my skin.

Leah hunches down over her phone, typing away as we take a seat where we have room around us. Me, I'm watching the surroundings and smelling the distinct aroma of burnt rubber. Cheers from the onlookers are loud as a bike gets ready to burn out. Usually, they lock their front tire, then rev the engine in an attempt to burn the tire off the back of the bike. They even have tire companies here that give them free tires for doing it.

I cover my ears as the noise grows from the bike and the crowd. The air fills with smoke as the cheers get even louder. More hollers, pats on the back, and money exchanging hands after the announcer states the rider's time.

Scanning the crowd, I don't spot my father, brothers, or anyone from Sinisters. Regardless, it's only a matter of time. They got back from their run yesterday, and we chatted a bit. I was surprised they never asked me about coming today. They left without a word, and so did I.

Looking down the way, my eyes connect with striking blue ones. The same ones I saw two days ago at the laundromat. Cooper.

He lifts a plastic cup to his lips, and I'm mesmerized by how they hold on to the rim as he drinks. His hair is disheveled, free and sexy as hell. He wears his black cut with a large group of men around him. A small smirk plays on his sexy lips, warming me from the inside out.

"There he is!" Leah says excitedly, hitting my arm.

I lose my contact with Cooper to turn and see who I'm assuming is Nick climbing up the bleachers, followed by two more men.

I lean into Leah. "If this is a set Bristyl up thing, I'm going to kill you."

"Go with it. They don't look bad."

Internally, I scoff. They sure as shit don't look like Cooper and his guys one bit. The first one has an intense stare, solely focused on my best friend. There's something behind those eyes that I don't like one little bit. He has on jeans, a white T-shirt, and a cut, but I can't see who he belongs to as I scan the patches.

One of the guys behind him has broad shoulders, a long, dark beard, and short, brown hair. His face is one that I've seen a million times. Nothing unique or different. The other guy, though, he is different. Blond hair that looks like it could use a wash and a scruff of beard. He is very tall, but built, if the definition of his arms says anything.

"Leah, you're more beautiful than the picture," Nick says smoothly. I want to rip his hand off as he touches her face seductively.

Leah gets all giddy from the attention, and I immediately recant my last thought, wanting to slap her over the damn head instead.

"Hi." Her girlish tone makes me wonder where my best friend went. What the hell? A guy comes along and she's suddenly a teenager with a crush? Seriously?

"These are my boys, Poe and Len." He motions to them then looks at me. "And you are?"

I still don't like the twinkle in his eye one little bit. I've been around too much in my life not to notice those small tells. My father taught me well. He may have shielded me from most of this life, but one can't live in it and not see or hear things.

"This is Bristyl," Leah happily tells them as the scary one, Poe, comes to sit by me, and way too closely, considering there is plenty of space for his ass to move down.

I study their cuts. Unlike Sinister Sons, they don't have a patch on the front telling what club they are from, only their names with a number. This is even more unsettling.

Oh, no, this shit isn't happening. My night is not going to be ruined because of these stupid assholes.

Poe puts his hand on my thigh like he has every right to, and I sit there, stunned for a brief moment. This man will not touch me, but if I do what I'm about to do, it could cause problems for Sinister.

I glance over to where Cooper is, his eyes now turned away from me. Great, he probably thinks I'm with this guy. What the hell do I care, anyway?

"Get your hands off me," I growl low as the asshole squeezes my thigh hard, causing a jolt of pain to slice through my leg.

My brain goes into survival mode, pulling up the things I learned over the years. I rip the guy's hand away, and he pinches me as he leaves my leg. Then I stand up quickly and move down a riser. Unfortunately, it doesn't give me a whole hell of a lot of distance.

"Come on, Leah, let's go," I tell my best friend, whose eyes are round in surprise. "Now," I bark.

She gets up, and Nick grabs her arm, pulling her back down to the seat. She struggles to get loose.

"Let me go," she cries as I reach up to grab her. As I do, Poe wraps his arm around my waist, and I pop him good in the shin with my foot. I feel it, too, only having flip flops on, but it's enough for him to loosen his hold on me to squirm away.

Nick stands. "Bitch, don't you know who we are?" He grips Leah's arm hard, and tears spring to her eyes. She hasn't grown up in this life, has only been my friend. This is going to get so much worse before it gets better if I don't get us out of this mess.

"I don't have a clue who you are. Now let go of her, and we'll go our way," I try to reason. Nick isn't having it.

"No, you're makin' a scene, so you're gonna come with us nicely so we don't get shit from anyone around us. Then I'll show you exactly who we are."

Fuck that.

"If I have to scream from the fucking rooftops, you better believe I will. We aren't going anywhere with you." I meet him head-on. Yeah, he will hurt me, but I'm not backing down, and there's no way in hell we are going anywhere with these men.

My heart hammers in my chest, but I force myself to keep cool. Not doing so will only make things even worse, as if they aren't bad enough already. Fuck me. Once we get out of this, I'm kicking Leah's ass.

CHAPTER EIGHT
Cooper

The laundromat girl is here. Or, more to the point, the woman. Damn, she's hotter than the damn devil, all wrapped up in sin. She has more clothes on than half the women here, yet looks a thousand times sexier. If anything, it's making me wonder what lies beneath the fabric.

Intrigue. That's exactly what it is.

Three assholes go up the risers, and her eyes turn from mine. In my gut, I want those eyes to look back.

The cuts on the backs of the men say Red Devils MC. We've had ties with them before, but nothing that warrants any concern.

Surveying the situation closer, the chick next to Bristyl knows the one guy, but from the body language Bristyl has no clue who any of these men are. It looks innocent enough, and it's not like she's mine, so why should I give a fuck?

Turning back to my brothers, we chat about stupid shit and drink. My eyes keep flickering back to Bristyl, though, and it doesn't go unnoticed.

"Oh … laundromat woman is here," Ryker says with a hint of humor. "Think she'll wanna see me again?"

Not sure why, but my blood boils. "No," is all I say.

"Oh, man, Coop, don't be doin' that shit."

"I'm not doin' a damn thing."

Just then, Bristyl jumps to her feet and down a bench. She grabs for her friend, but the asshole next to her pulls her back down. From here, I can see tears in her friend's eyes. This shit isn't my business, but I'm making it.

"Come," I tell Ryker, who taps Green and Jacks.

"Where you goin', boy?" my dad calls out.

I just point to Bristyl and keep moving through the crowd. I feel my brothers at my back, just like they always are.

Bristyl is arguing with the guys from the way her hands are moving, along with her head. I can only see the back of it, but it reminds me of my mom when she's giving shit to my dad.

I climb the risers and get right behind Bristyl. "There a problem here?"

Bristyl turns abruptly, breaths coming in surprised pants. I don't take my eyes from the guys in front of me, though, no matter how much I'd rather look at her.

"Cooper," she whispers so softly I don't think she meant to say it out loud, and damn, it's so sensuous that my cock hardens.

"These are our bitches. Go find your own." The asshole has his hand wrapped around Bristyl's friend so tightly his knuckles are white. He rises, taking her with him, and she screeches, trying to pull her arm from his grasp as he begins to pull her away from Bristyl.

Bristyl moves so damn fast I can't even catch her. One second she's in front of me. The next, she's between the asshole and her friend, full-on biting the guy's arm.

"Holy fuck," Green says from behind me.

The asshole pulls back, letting go of the friend and lifting his other hand, ready to strike Bristyl across the face. It's my turn to be quick.

Grabbing Bristyl, I maneuver her behind me and slug the guy in the gut, then in the jaw. He staggers back. I hear my brothers behind me, no doubt taking on the other two.

"What's going on?" my father asks, coming up and grabbing the punk by the collar.

"Assholes are putting their hands on women who don't want to be touched," I tell him.

"Let's move this away from prying eyes."

The crowd is all in for a fight, amped up on the energy, feeding off our conflict. Fuck, this could turn seriously bad. Nothing worse than a rally full of bikers who turn all out for blood. Too many dead bodies and way too many fucking questions.

"Bristyl, you and your friend follow us."

She nods, wrapping her arm around her friend as we lug the three assholes down the bleachers and out the back way. We get quite a few stares, so Dagger jokes with some of the onlookers, putting them at ease. Never met a man who could simmer shit down like that man. I tried to pick up that skill, but haven't quite mastered it yet.

"Talk," Pops says, coming up to my side as I toss the asshole to the ground. Rhys blocks him from going anywhere, making me regret how we aren't on our home turf.

"Asshole was putting his hands on the girls. Wouldn't leave 'em alone."

"And this is our business why?" he asks, looking down at the two girls who are sitting on a small bench. Bristyl has her arms around her friend, holding her as she cries. Bristyl doesn't cry, though. No, she has fire burning in her eyes. Anger. Revenge. Damn, that gets me hard.

"Know her. She helped us out at the laundromat."

"And still, Coop, this has nothing to do with us. Bringin' shit to our door that doesn't need to be."

I look to my grandfather, my president, staring into his eyes, not sure what I'm trying to tell him, but his eyes flash in some type of recognition.

"Son of a motherfucker. Alright," he says, lifting his hand and spinning his finger. "Can't do much, too many eyes. Just make sure they get the fuck out of here. I'll talk to their prez."

This is Ravage. I may not have fallen in line according to our lifestyle, but the club takes my back whether I'm right or wrong.

Buzz, Breaker, Tug, Becs, and GT "help" the guys out as I move over to Bristyl, who hasn't taken her eyes off the dickheads as they leave.

"Green." I nod over to the girl. He's always been good with emotional women.

He makes his move over to them, and Bristyl turns her angry gaze on him. I want to laugh because she looks like she's about to pounce on Green, and that shit would be funny. Not that he couldn't hold his own, but it'd still be funny for her to try.

I move up. "Bristyl, come here so I can find out what happened."

She surveys the situation, but doesn't leave her friend's side. Gotta respect her loyalty.

"Promise nothin's gonna happen to her," Pops says, coming closer.

Her eyes dart to him, then down to his rag. She's no doubt seeing the word "*President*," but it's a toss-up on which way she'll go.

"I'm Pops. Cooper's grandpa and the president of Ravage MC. I get you're scared, but we need to talk to ya for a bit."

Her eyes get sharp and narrow into slits. "I'm not scared. I'm pissed as hell."

"Obviously, she's breathin' fire," Dagger says.

"You hit on me earlier," she responds.

"I did? Fuck, my ol' lady's gonna cut my dick off."

Her face softens just a touch. "You said that earlier, too."

"We're not here to hurt you, but I need to know what shit we've gotten ourselves into, Bristyl," I tell her, hoping she can put the claws away just for a few minutes. Hell, I like that she has them. I like that she doesn't put up with the bullshit, and that she fucking bit the guy to get her friend loose. She was damn ready to take the backhand if it meant her friend was out of that asshole's grasp. She definitely has loyalty.

"Leah, I need to talk to these guys. Breathe. Everything's gonna be fine. I'll deal with this, and then we'll get the fuck out of here," she consoles her friend, unlatching herself from the woman's grasp. Then she walks over to me as Green slips in. I have no doubt he'll have her friend laughing in a matter of minutes.

I scan her body, noting the large red mark on her thigh. No man puts his hands on a woman like that. Respect goes two ways. You don't respect a woman, then she won't respect you. It could be for a night or longer, but it's a two-way street, and both of you need to be on board for it to work. Here, that didn't happen.

She crosses her arms, pushing her pert breasts up, which doesn't help my already hard cock.

"Hi," she says softly in that purr.

"Hey, wanna tell me what happened?"

Her eyes dart around like she's looking for someone, then comes back to me. "Leah met Nick on this dating website. She set it up to meet him here. The little tart actually sprang it on me on the way here. I told her it was a shit idea, but she had already told him we were going to be here. Nick came up to her, and I could tell they were assholes right away. The guy next to me, Poe, only said a couple of words to me before his hand was on my thigh. I got pissed and jumped away when his grip tightened. Nick grabbed Leah's arm when I tried to pull her with me, and then you showed up."

"And you bit the fucker's arm."

"I'm lucky I didn't draw blood. Can you imagine having that asshole's taste on my tongue?" Her body full-out shivers. "I'm sorry you got involved, but thank you for your help."

Laughter comes from the small bench, and Bristyl whips around. Green's done his job. Her friend is laughing at something he said and warming up to him.

Him and his ways. He may have been green, but he's always had a way with women.

I turn back toward Bristyl. "You do realize you're at a biker rally, right?"

"I'm here to see a band." She turns toward Pops. "Look, I'm sorry. We're going to get out of here."

"Green and Coop will walk you to your car," Pops decrees. I couldn't have said it better myself.

While teaching those assholes a lesson is ideal, the view of Bristyl is a thousand times better. I got in a few good shots if my bloody knuckles are anything to go by. That will have to do … for now.

Green wraps his arm around Leah, and she goes willingly, no longer the scared mouse from moments ago. She's attractive, don't get me wrong, but the blonde beside me has her beat by a mile.

Bristyl walks next to me, her hands in the back pockets of her shorts, her eyes scanning the place.

"My brothers got them out," I reassure her as she looks up at me with those startling blue eyes, round and sucking me in like a cyclone.

"I know."

"Then why're you so jumpy?"

"Just on guard." She shrugs it off, but I can feel it's something. And for some reason, I let her get away with it.

She takes a few steps in front of me. Her round ass has the perfect sway as she walks. I notice men and women alike looking at her. She has this striking quality that I don't think she sees in herself by the easy way she acts.

Getting through the crowds, Bristyl leads me down a hill, and then farther away from the rally. "You ladies walked this far?"

"Yeah, parking was a bitch."

"And you were going to walk this far, in the dark, by yourself?"

She seems like a really smart woman, yet that just screams "kill me."

"It doesn't matter now because we have you." When she looks up at me and smiles, the air leaves my lungs. Having that much power directed right at me is a shot to the heart. Not once in my life has this happened. Not once has a woman grabbed my attention so completely. Never once have I realized that a woman is way too good for a man like me. She's too good and doesn't need to get mixed up in the biker lifestyle. Even seeing her go after the guy and biting him, and having spunk, she can do so much better. Even for one night. Even for a quickie in the back of her car. Hell, even for a lifetime of those smiles.

Bristyl deserves better than me.

"Here we are." She pulls out her keys and bleeps the locks, making the interior of the car come to life.

Green walks Leah to the passenger side while I walk Bristyl to the driver's.

As she turns and looks up at me, her eyes swirl. "Thank you for everything."

One taste. I want one taste. Is she as sweet as she looks, or is the sin tart to the tongue?

She brings her hands up to my chest, the heat from them sending a shock all the way down to my toes. Then she licks her bottom lip before placing it between her teeth. She wants to kiss me, too, and is giving me the go-ahead.

With the willpower of every fucking superhero ever created, I pull her into my arms, resting her head on my chest. I inhale the scent of some type of flower, burning it to memory. If I kiss her, if I taste her, I won't be able to stop myself. That's not weakness, it's reality.

Giving her another squeeze and using every bit of restraint within myself, I step back out of her grasp, and she looks up at me in confusion.

"You take care of yourself, Bristyl. Don't get messed up in this world. You're too good."

She goes to say something, but I raise my hand.

"Be safe." I turn and walk away, up the hill and to my brothers who have gotten rid of the problem.

"You mean to tell me that we took on this shit and you're not even gonna claim her?" my father roars as we're about to enter the hotel later that night.

I'd already told him what happened and how I played it. Not only is he my father, but my brother as well, and I owe him the truth on both counts.

After Bristyl drove away, I felt a small place inside me turn cold. Even all the pussy in the world couldn't make it warm, so I decided to go to bed.

"It's better this way." I slip the card into the door and open it, my father right on my heels.

"Stay," he orders Green, who came back with me. Then my father shuts the door and turns the deadbolt.

I toss my keys, wallet, and some junk from my pockets onto the small, round table by the window. Every hotel I've ever been in has the same damn things—bed, TV, dresser, chair, and a stupid little table in front of the window.

"Why the fuck are you saying that?"

This isn't the first time my father's been angry with me, and it won't be the last. His lifetime quota has yet to be met. I can't blame him, either. Although a member, he will always be my father. The choices I make are a reflection of him whether I want them to or not. It's how the world works.

I fall into the chair and it creaks from my weight. "Dad, look, she lives here in Florida—"

"And?"

"I'm not gonna have her hop on the back of my bike and take her to Sumner when she has no fuckin' clue what she's gettin' herself into."

"How do you know that? She was at the rally, son." He sits in the chair across from me.

I shrug. "Somethin' about her screamed innocent in a way. Or, not tainted from the life. She needs to stay far away from us bikers. I mean, hell, she works at a laundromat for Christ's sake. That screams clean."

He sits back in the chair and crosses his arms over his wide chest. His caramel colored hair is getting darker and shows a few gray hairs, but I'm blaming those on my brother and sister. When I was younger, I thought he could move mountains, was the coolest person in the entire world, and wanted to be him when I grew up. Now I am. I'm not the coolest person, but like him—strong, determined, and smart.

He swipes his hand over the scruff of his beard and down his face.

"So, what, you're gonna go home and drown yourself in pussy and booze?"

"If I want to." Booze doesn't sound half-bad at the moment.

"When I met your mother, I held a gun to her head."

"I know this."

"But what you don't know is that I claimed her the moment our eyes locked. Come hell or high water, that woman was going to be mine. I didn't give her a choice. Of course, she could have beat the hell out of me, or at least tried." He chuckles. "The point is, when you know, you know. But you're young and have your whole life ahead of you. You sure as shit don't need to be settling down anytime soon." My father latches his fingers and places his hands behind his head as I take in his words.

I have no plans of settling down. It was just a feeling I had when she was near me. It doesn't mean shit.

"I'm not."

"But, you find the one that makes your life whole, better not fuck that up. That'll be your biggest regret. Young or not, I taught you to think about everything—every angle." I let his words penetrate deeply. "Enough of this heart to heart shit. Get some shut eye. We're leavin' at eight."

"Got it."

My father rises from the chair, stretches, then heads to the door. "And, son?"

"Yeah."

"Life will lead you where you need to be, or you need to man up and lead it where you want it to go." He turns toward the door and walks out, his message remaining in my thoughts.

CHAPTER NINE

Bristyl

Stomping out of my office, my temper is on fire, and Stone is my target. The mechanic shop is fully stocked with everything one would need, and it's the top place my brother will be. I've had enough of his shit. Hell, I've had enough with a lot of things; he's just on top of the list. Lucky him.

"Stone!" My voice is loud, garnering the attention of pretty much everyone in the place, including my father, but that doesn't stop me.

"What?" he barks back, wiping his hands off on a greasy towel. The classic Plymouth Barracuda is looking nice, but I'm not telling him that. He's been restoring it for ages, working on it whenever he has down time.

"I fucking told you to give. Me. The. Receipts! I'm missing twelve! Twelve, Stone! I've had it. I keep asking and keep asking, and do you do what I ask? No! You completely ignore me to the point that, right now, I have to go to the bank and straighten the books out, because they don't want to do that many over the phone!"

I'm fully aware I'm losing my shit, but there's been a lot on my mind the past couple of weeks. The main one: a man who shouldn't be in my head, but won't go away and leave me alone. Instead, he invades my dreams. He's always there. When I close my eyes, when I take a shower—hell, when I drive to work! I'm losing my mind. It has to be the case, because this shit isn't right.

Add in Leah calling me four, five, six times a day, apologizing for what happened, even though I told her it's all over now. She's disconnected her online dating thingy and even changed her phone number to make sure Nick can't find her. Thank God she didn't give him her address and faked a last name. At least she was thinking there. The *I'm sorry's* are getting old. Like, way old.

Then this damn bruise on my leg. I didn't think it was that bad, but the asshole really grabbed me hard, leaving his handprint that turned a greenish purple. Wearing jeans for a week to cover it in this warm weather hasn't made me happy, either, but no way will my father or brothers find out. It's over and in the past.

Mr. Draker finished what he said he would, but he didn't put in enough shutoffs, so now he has to go in and redo it. I mean, how fucking hard is it? Six machines, twelve shutoffs. Six hot, six cold. Done. If I knew how to solder a pipe, my ass would be over there fixing it myself.

Everything is just piling on top of each other, and these receipts have put me over the edge. It feels like I can't catch my breath.

"Calm down, Bristyl," Stone snaps, pissing me off more.

"Do you want to go to the bank and sit with that mean teller who has the personality skills of a gnat? Want to sit across from him and go line by line on the credit statement? Because if you do, I'll be more than happy to let you," I fire back.

"I have the receipts, just calm your shit."

"All of them?"

"Yes. What's crawled up your ass lately? The past week or two, you've been a royal bitch."

My skin prickles. I can feel the top on the kettle about to blow, allowing the steam to rupture.

Several guys around Stone's car stop to stare at us, but I'm too pissed off to give a shit. The fucks have all gone.

"You …" I take a step closer to Stone, getting in his face.

A steel-banded arm wraps around my waist, and I turn to see my father who picks me up.

"Kiss my ass!" I scream as my father shuts the door to my office with a loud crash after pushing me inside, my hair flying this way and that.

"What is your problem? You don't act like this, Bristyl!" he fires at me, and it feels like a physical slap. My father, the big brute he is, rarely raises his voice. And more rarely raises his voice to me. He's calm most of the time, but in this moment, he's anything but.

"I'm just frustrated." I rip my fingers through my hair and pull a chuck of it hard, leaving them to rest on top of my head. "I can't do my job when they don't do what they're supposed to do. I've had it!"

"You quitin'?"

Startled by his words, I suck in a huge breath then let it out slowly. The anger fades, and my temper cools a touch.

"No, Dad. All I want is the receipts so I can do what I have to do. I hate going down to the bank because it makes me look incompetent at my job. Then it makes the club look bad because your name is on all the paperwork."

He falls into the chair.

Taking a closer look at him, there are circles under his eyes that seemed to have taken up residence since he and my brothers returned from their run before the rally. The wrinkle on his forehead has deepened a bit and the lines around his mouth.

"You'll have all the paperwork you need. On each Friday, I'll have the boys bring you your shit. That solve it?"

Leaning against the wall, I plop my head back on the concrete block, letting every bit of anger release from my body. In its place, a twinge of worry forms. "Yeah, thanks."

"Gotta chat."

That catches my attention.

I move to my chair, take a seat, and fold my hands in front of me. Whatever this is, maybe it has to do with the change in my father. It piques my curiosity, yet terrifies me.

"That shit out there in the garage will *never* happen again. You think doing that shit in front of anyone is okay? You're damn lucky those are brothers out there and not paying people, or your ass would be in a shitload deeper. You're not a member of this club. You're not an ol' lady. You're an employee, and you need to learn your place. I've been really lenient on you, but after that little tantrum out there, you need to realize where you stand. Gotta toe the fuckin' line, Bristyl. Keep your shit in check."

I'm pretty sure, if my father took a knife and shoved it in my chest, twisting it around, it would have hurt less. My entire life has been about the Sinister Sons. When my mom was alive, she let me tag along with her, all the while I only wanted to be a part of this family. My brothers were engrossed in it. My dad let them come to the club all the time with him, but said I couldn't.

I didn't understand at the time. When my mother told me it was because my gender and girls don't become members of the club, I cut my pigtails off so I'd have short hair like a boy. I think I was six or so. It was totally irrational, but being so young, belonging meant everything to me. It didn't work, of course.

My life has revolved around cookouts, brothers coming to our house, and charity runs where I'd ride on the back of my dad's bike because my mom didn't want to go. All of it felt like I belonged, but in the end, I don't. I've never fit in anywhere here, and that realization is a punch to the gut.

In my heart, I always knew it, but never thought about it, taking the avoidance route. Regardless, my father is right. I'm not a part of this. I'm an employee who happens to be the vice president's daughter and sister to three members. That's it. However, it's the fact that my father thinks that way that hurts most of all.

Tears sting the backs of my eyes, but I refuse to let them fall. No way in hell. I'm stronger than everyone gives me credit for. Stronger than this hurt. If anything, it's making me realize that I somehow need to carve out a life for myself, one that doesn't include Sinisters. Would that exclude my family, too?

I clear my throat before answering, keeping my tone as low and calm as possible, not allowing an ounce of the hurt to shine through. "I've got it. Can I call the bank please and tell them that I won't be coming?"

My father shakes his head. "I'll have Stone bring the receipts, and you can apologize to him."

The hole in my heart grows wider. Not only do I get reprimanded, told I'm not a part of the family I love and have supported, but now I have to apologize? Great, just great. And if I don't do it, I have no idea what my father will do. Judging from his demeanor, I don't want to find out, either.

My bed is cold when I climb into it, the sheets cooling my overheated skin. After apologizing to my brother and entering all the receipts, I came home.

Home. It's not so much that anymore with my mother gone. She left a hole so deep that the warmth she had disappeared. I don't stop the tears from rolling down my face as I allow myself to miss her. So. Damn. Much. She would've had the advice I need. She would've pointed me in a direction. She would've put her hand out, yanked me out, and stopped me from drowning. She would've guided me or talked to my father and see where all of this is coming from.

Grabbing the pillow, I tuck it close to me and cry myself to sleep.

Instead of calling in sick the next day and avoiding work altogether, I go in, do my job, am cordial to people and leave as if yesterday never happened. I get weird looks, and my brothers stay clear of me. There is no way I will let them see they got to me. Not happening. The day goes by quickly, thank God.

As I sit in my living room, twirling my phone, thoughts run rampant.

"You take care of yourself, Bristyl. Don't get messed up in this world. You're too good. Be safe." Cooper's last words to me make me want to laugh. He doesn't have a clue that I'm in this shit as far as a woman can get without being in it. Father a VP, brothers are members, Mom was an ol' lady. I'm too good? Too good for what, exactly? For him? Please.

He has no idea that I grew up with the Sinister Sons. That thought makes me pause, because I kind of like it. I like that I don't have my association with the Sinisters hanging over my head. I've been asked on plenty of dates, but I never get a second date because my brothers scare the piss out of them.

They always say, *"Any man who takes my sister out had better be able to stand up to us and show his worth."* Cooper would. He wouldn't back down from them. He's that kind of man; I can feel it in my bones. From the way he was at the rally, making sure we were safe, I know he wouldn't back down from anyone.

I swipe my thumb over the screen of my phone and go to the recent calls, scrolling down until I find a Georgia number. The same number that called me from the laundromat.

When people call me, they don't realize they are getting my cell phone. They figure it's a landline, but what's the point? Unlimited minutes and all. Not only that, I really don't get that many calls, and most of the time, they go to voicemail and I return their messages later.

My finger hovers over the number like a magnet, urging me to push it, so I click. A screen pops up with a phone and an envelope. I choose the envelope. Text messaging first. Why not?

I type, *Hey, it's me. Bristyl.* Then delete it.

It's Bristyl from the rally.

Delete.

I'm thinking of you.

Delete fast.

Fucking hell, what's wrong with me? I feel like a damn teenager, afraid to talk to a boy for the first time. All my thoughts turn into a mangled mess of words.

I type, *Hi.* Then, before I chicken out, I press my thumb down, sending the message. My damn hands begin to sweat as I wonder if he will text me back or blow me off. He more than likely didn't save my number in his phone, so he has no clue who it is.

I'm seriously losing it. I met the guy twice. Twice, and I'm acting like a damn fool.

A few moments later, I get a, *Who is this?*

I reply with shaky fingers, *Bristyl*

I wait for a response.

And wait.

And wait.

When it doesn't come, I toss my phone on the table and click on the television. I guess that's that. Can't say part of me isn't let down. It is. Expecting any differently than what I got, though, is on me.

Bye, Cooper.

CHAPTER TEN
Cooper

Five hours later, Bristyl's name still stares back at me from my phone. And hell yeah, shocked doesn't even begin to describe what I'm feeling. I thought I called a business phone. Wrong.

Two weeks, and the woman still won't get out of my head. It's like she's glued and has adhered herself to me in a strange way. Now here she is, contacting me.

Rubbing my hand over my face, I collapse on the bed. The clubhouse is calm tonight. I didn't want to go home with Ryker, Green, and Jacks. We rent a house five minutes from the clubhouse, each having our own space. That doesn't mean that they leave me alone. I needed some time to myself to digest this sudden turn of events.

It's funny because, last week, I thought about taking a drive down to Florida after a long-haired blonde came to the club and Bristyl immediately came to mind. Instead, I took a ride, needing to clear my head. Something kept me close to home.

Looking at her name on my phone, my finger hoovers over her name. That connection I felt with her, was it the moment or something else?

My father's words haunt me. He's right. Damn.

I type: *Hey, are you there?*

The clock reads midnight, so the chances of her responding are slim, especially if she has to get up and work tomorrow.

What do you want? Surprisingly, my phone lights up with her response, and I chuckle, liking her direct tone.

To talk.

That sounds so dumb. Having a conversation with a female over text is a new thing for me. If the guys knew, they would razz the shit out of me and I'd probably end up punching one of them.

B: I'm sleeping.
Me: No, you're not.
B: I was.
Me: Now you're awake. How are you?

My phone turns to black as I wait for her text. I kick my boots off and move up the bed, resting my head on the pillow, arm behind my head, holding the phone with the other.

B: Tired, but fine.
Me: Any explosions of water lately?
B: ☺ No, thank goodness.

A goofy-ass smile spreads across my face. All I can do is picture her in a damn wet T-shirt, cleaning up all the water. Damn, now I'm hard.

Me: Tell me something about you.
B: Like?

Shit, what do I want to know? I'm not used to actually asking a woman questions about herself. Hell, sometimes I don't even get a name. That may make me a dick, but it is what it is. This is so out of left field for me, I should be in a different state. Maybe Florida.

My brother and sister come to mind.

Me: Do you have any siblings?
B: Three brothers.
Me: Damn, beat me. I have a brother and a sister—twins.

B: *That's kinda cool.*
Me: *They're good kids, but a pain in the ass.*
B: *I know the feeling.*

I sit there for a while, liking the conversation and trying to think of what to say next. Are you a true blonde? Definitely not asking that. Are your tits real? If this goes any further, I'll find that out myself … Fuck.

Me: *Why did you text me?*

There's a long pause, and the screen goes black again. It's an honest question that I'd like to know the answer to. Have I been on her mind? Does she dream of me? Or am I just a biker for her to get her kicks on with. Okay, so I don't believe that last one because she would have acted differently with me at the rally. Damn if I can get my mind to stop reeling.
The phone lights up.

B: *I've been thinking about you.*

Strange how those five little words fill me with happiness.

Me: *Oh yeah?*
B: *Yeah.*
Me: *Care to tell me more?*
B: *Not really.*

I full-out laugh, loving the way she says what she wants. That spark in her is an attraction I can't hide.

Me: *You're making me bust a gut here.*
B: *Am I that funny?*
Me: *Yeah, and cute.*
B: *I'm not cute.*
Me: *Yes, you are.*
B: *No, I'm not.*
Me: *Yes, you are.*
B: *Are we really going to argue about whether I'm cute or not? Which I'm not.*

Hell yes, she is. Even over texting. I can only imagine her in person or on the phone.

Flirting. That's exactly what I'm doing, and it feels damn good.

Me: Yes, I like it.
B: You like arguing with me?
Me: What did you do after the rally?
B: Way to avoid.

I write nothing back and wait, wanting to know exactly what she did. The thought of some asshole getting with her doesn't sit right with me one bit.

B: Dropped off Leah and went home.
Me: Home to ...
B: You're baiting me.
Yes. Yes, I am. I need to know.
B: To my house, ALONE.

At that, I reach over to my small nightstand and grab my old baseball. I lay flat on the bed, toss it up into the air, then catch it. It's been a long damn time since I played. Luckily for me, I can text with one hand.

Me: Damn shame.
B: I'm used to it.
Me: Being alone?
B: Yep.
Me: Are your parents around?

I'm not sure why, but her saying that she's alone doesn't sit right in my gut. Her not having someone for any reason pisses me off. She has brothers, but are they not around or do they live all over the place?

B: My dad is.

I relate to this a lot. I have to ask ...

Me: Your mom?

B: Died.

The ball drops to the bed as I stare blankly at the ceiling. Funny how this part of our lives is similar. What are the odds?

Me: Damn, babe. Sorry.
B: It's the circle of life or whatever.

The urge to tell her about my situation hits me. I never shared that part of me with any woman before, and I'm not sure doing it over text is the right thing. It's a bit heavy. Not everyone can handle the fucked-up story of my biological mother who didn't care for me and ended up dead because she was stupid. My father only told me the full story when I got older. Truthfully, the entire thing only allowed me to appreciate my mother, Princess, all that much more.

It's strange even contemplating talking to her about it. Deep inside, the words want to come out.

Me: Remind me sometime to tell you my story.
B: You assume there'll be a next time.
Me: I can promise you that.

The feeling swirling inside of me from this one conversation feels too damn good to not have again.

B: My eyes are drooping. I need sleep.
Me: Get some sleep, beautiful.
B: Night.

I fall asleep with Bristyl on my mind.

Chaos surrounds me like a shroud of darkness. The weight on top of me pushes my small body hard into the linoleum floor of the clubhouse. All the while, screams echo the space.

Leggs slaps a hand over my mouth and whispers in my ear, "Shh … Cooper. You've gotta stay really quiet." Her weight holds me down to the point I can't move my legs or arms.

I squirm, wanting to get free.

I look around, lifting up to see a man holding a gun to my grandma's head. He's yelling, or at least with my one ear covered it sounds like it.

Fear hits me as the man holds the gun out, aims, and fires. The sound is loud and cracks like a whip.

My head jerks to the side as I watch my mother fall to the ground with dark red blood coming out of her leg.

"No!" the words are muffled by a hand that grips tighter, Leggs' words for me to be quiet ignored.

I use every bit of strength from my tiny body to try to get free, wishing I was big like my dad, then I could move.

My mom is only a little bit away from me. I just need to get to her.

Tears spring from my eyes as she holds her leg, making sounds she shouldn't be making. No, Mommy!

I bolt up from bed, gasping then blinking. A light sheen of sweat coats my skin.

Rubbing my hand over my face, the memories cling to me like a dark cloak. In that moment, I knew I'd do anything to protect those I love. Whatever price. Whatever it took. My family comes first. We are bound together. If I could only shake the dreams.

The Ravage MC has two businesses. Besides Studio X, we have Banner Automotive. I work at both, but mostly at the shop. Since the time I could hold a damn wrench in my hand, my dad taught me how to work on bikes, cars, trucks—hell, anything with a motor. Luckily for me, my skillset is good at picking up shit quick.

Angel, GT's ol' lady, Deke's mom, and my aunt, brought her '56 Chevy in today for an oil and transmission fluid change. She insisted on helping, having once worked here when she was younger, hanging tough with all the guys. She knows her way around any type of engine. After Deke was born, though, she hung up her rags. Still, she comes in whenever her car needs something.

She loves that thing. Her and her dad Bam restored it. Bam was a member of the club, but died years ago. She keeps that car for the sentimental value.

She has a minivan, too. I think it's hilarious seeing GT drive the beast. It gives all of us something to razz him about. His big-ass body climbing in and out of that minivan is a sight.

Angel works while I stand back and watch. Once she gets going, it's best to just leave her be. She just pushes us out of the way, anyway.

Hell, it's her car, so why do I give a shit?

My phone vibrates in my pocket. I pull it out, seeing *"Bristyl"* on the screen, and swipe the screen as the excitement hits. Damn, this is strange.

B: *How's your day?*
Me: *Working. You?*
B: *Me, too.*
Me: *At the laundromat?*

I look around the garage, seeing everyone busy, including Angel, which is a good thing. No one needs to know about Bristyl.

B: *And the storage units.*
Me: *? Damn, you're busy.*
B: *Always.*
Me: *You have storage units, too?*

Storage units. That rolls around in my head. Empty spaces to rent out would be good if Ravage needs to store anything. That could be a possibility to our situation.

B: *Yeah, about an acre of land with 220 of them.*
Me: *Damn.*

My thoughts run with the storage unit idea. This could be what we need.

"Girlfriend?" Angel asks, wiping her hands on a cloth.

I stuff my phone in my back pocket, not realizing exactly how much time has gone by while my eyes have been glued to my damn phone. "Nah."

"I call bullshit. I don't think I've see that goofy-ass smile on your face before. Who is she?"

I look around, making sure none of the guys are around to hear me. One word of a woman, and I have no doubt that any of the brothers would put it together. It's nothing, and I don't need shit for it.

"No one. Keep your mouth shut."

Her brow quirks. "Oh, man, you've got it bad."

I get up in her space. "I mean it. Don't give me shit, and do not tell

GT."

She uses her index finger and thumb to show me she's zipping her lips, all the while wearing a smile on her lips. That's about as good as I'm going to get with her.

Shit, it's only a matter of time before my mother, Angel's best friend, finds out. Too bad duct taping ol' ladies' mouths isn't an option.

"Come on, let's finish this."

Me: Call me.

This text was sent to her about ten minutes ago, and not a word. It's only eight, so I don't think she's sleeping. We did the text thing off and on throughout the day, but I'm over it. I want to talk to her and have a real conversation. One where her purring voice comes through the line, and I can distinguish her jokes, sarcasm, and seriousness without having to guess all the damn time.

The house we live in is your typical bachelor pad. Everything is industrial because shit gets broken more times than not. Hell, our coffee table, Green and I made it out of two-by-fours and sheets of plywood to make sure it was strong. I can't tell you how many times Ryker has jumped on top of it when the Bulldogs scored a touchdown or won a game. It holds sound every damn time.

The couches are used and abused. We got them from Green's parents, who were getting new ones. They're comfortable, and that's all that really matters. The best thing in the space is our eighty-inch television, which is in the center of the wall with all the couches facing it.

We have a couple of beer posters up on the wall, but not much else. The white is a bit dirty now that I look at it. We may need to repaint it at some point.

It's not home. It's more of a place to crash when we aren't at the club. A home is like the place my mom and dad have, where I grew up.

Listen to me. I should smack myself in the head. Why my thoughts are going this way is up for debate.

"Bro! Heads-up!" Ryker calls out as he tosses a bag of chips my way.

I catch them with ease. Opening them up, I pop a barbecue flavored chip in my mouth.

"Wanna head out tonight?" he asks, plopping down on the couch next to me, grabbing the bag and taking some chips.

I think about Bristyl and wonder if she's going to call. Maybe I should give her just a little more time before making any plans.

"Maybe later. I just need to chill."

"Cool." He shoves more chips into his mouth. "You think any more about the different businesses to approach the club with?"

Hell yes. The car wash was a good idea, but the moving parts are my hang up.

Bristyl. That's my new idea. I'm actually stealing it from her. I began my search for information on it. It's damn near perfect, and it will work all the way around. Storage units. It can be all cash for the most part, and we could put fencing around the place so the renters would need a security code to get onto the property. This way, it won't have to be manned twenty-four seven, and Buzz can hook it up with security. I haven't worked out all the details yet, but it's definitely workable. My goal for the club is to work smarter, not harder.

"Yeah, I think I'm going to bring it up to my dad first and see what he thinks. Then go from there." I gave Ryker, Green, and Jacks a bit of a heads-up on my thoughts, but I haven't told them any of my plans yet. Making sure it's feasible before giving it to the club is important to me.

"Good idea," he mumbles around a mouthful of chips. "He'll give it to ya straight."

Damn right he will.

My phone begins to ring. Bristyl. She fucking called back, and the stupid-ass grin on my face cannot be stopped.

"Be back in a few." I charge into my room and lock the door, knowing Ryker's nosy-ass will be in here if I don't.

CHAPTER ELEVEN

Bristyl

Nerves hit me like a lead weight. I'm actually calling him. It seems weird that my anxiety is so high, considering we have been texting for a few days now. But with texting, I can think about what I'm saying and erase it quickly if it's stupid. Which I took advantage of a lot in our chats.

Talking directly is a bit intimidating, knowing I'll fuck up. That's just me. I guess he better learn sooner rather than later that stupid shit flies out of my mouth before I can catch it pretty much eighty percent of the time.

The phone rings … and rings … and rings, and right when I think it's going to voicemail, I hear, "Hello?" in the sexiest deep voice. It's like velvet, soft yet, if you rub it the other way, a bit rough. The sound causes my skin to prickle in a delectable way.

"Hey," comes out breathy, and I immediately want to smack myself.

Good job, Bristyl, going for the sexy voice. Perfect. Even clearing my throat doesn't get rid of it.

"You wanted me to call?" See, right there, stupid. *Duh, you're talking to him on the phone, you dork!*

I need my brain checked or transplanted. Probably both at this point.

He chuckles, and it warms me inside. "Yeah, texts are gettin' a bit much. Not that I don't like hearin' from ya, but I'm more of a talk guy."

"I figured that."

"Oh, you did. Why's that?"

My brain screams, *because you seem to be an action man, and texting is more of a passive thing*, but it would be stupid tossing every card I have out on the table so early.

I begin to pace, looking down and noting some of the fluff has gone out of the carpet. "I don't know, just the way you were at the rally. You seem to be in the moment."

His laughter comes over the line, sending goose bumps down my arms. Damn, I like that.

"Somethin' like that."

"Yeah, something." I sigh heavily, feeling like an idiot. "Look, I'm not good at this."

"What a coincidence, neither am I."

"You're not?" This surprises me. I mean, come on, Cooper is a hot man. He must have women all over. That thought twists my gut.

"Beautiful, I'm a biker; we don't chat with women."

No, they don't. They sleep with them and then move on to the next. I saw my brothers do it when they still lived in the house.

The idea of Cooper getting serviced by another woman sends burning fire through my veins. It's not that I don't like it …

I hate it.

After a pause, I'm relieved when he talks. "So, today I was at the shop."

"Banner, right?"

"You paid attention."

Boy, have I ever. Every little tidbit of information he gives me, I suck on it, wanting to know every detail.

"I was there with Ryker today," he continues, "and this asshole comes in, demanding to get his car fixed immediately. He was one of those suit wearin' types who has an office job and has never gotten his hands dirty in his life. Well, this doesn't fly well. We get into an argument, and he calls me a pussy bitch."

I laugh. "I bet that went over well."

"Let's just say the asshole won't ever come back."

"I bet not. I've seen the guys you hang out with."

"My brothers."

"Yeah, your brothers." My mind spins at this revelation. It's not that I didn't know; it just hadn't sunk in. Cooper has brothers, just like my blood does. They see me as an outcast. The pain hits me that Cooper would think the same thing. I'm in their world, but not. I know some things, but not most. I'm an outsider looking in. Cooper is going to realize that soon enough, and our conversations are going to be over.

Dread washes over me like a cold shower.

Is this a premonition of what's to come? Hell, I barely know the guy. I shouldn't even care, but I do. Dammit.

"Where'd ya go?"

I snap back to the conversation. "I'm here."

"Nah, you were far away."

"Sorry, it was a busy day." It's not a lie, but it isn't the entire truth, either.

"Tell me about it."

"Paperwork is a huge part of my day and keeping track of all the money, dealing with complaints." A poof of air comes up as I fall to my bed, phone attached to my ear.

"What's a funny complaint you get?"

"The funniest was"—I start laughing, unable to hold it back—"a customer called because the washer she put her seven dildos in broke every single one of them."

He bursts out laughing. "You're shittin' me?"

"Nope. She wanted us to replace all of them, saying they were hundreds of dollars. Which hell, they could've been, but there's no way I'm paying to replace a woman's vibrators because she was too stupid and put them in a washing machine. I mean, come on, they're electronic for the most part, and you're soaking them in water! Not only that, hello! The spin cycle. It had to have made a hell of a noise."

"That would've been funnier than shit to see."

"Oh, I bet. She was bitchin' and yellin' up a storm over the phone. Cussing me up and down."

"What'd ya do?"

"Hung up on her."

"That's not very good customer relations." He doesn't have to tell me that.

"Nope, it's not. I called her a few hours later, after she blew up my phone. Then, after I called her, I blocked her number. When we talked, I explained that she needed to look on the packaging of her *equipment* and see the proper cleaning instructions. Because, I know damn well it doesn't say throw them in washing machine on the spin cycle." I laugh. "She told me she was going to turn us in to the Better Business Bureau. Whoopee. Can you see that complaint on the BBB website? *I put my vibrators in one of their washing machines, and it broke them all. The witch on the phone said they weren't responsible for my stupidity. Then my question is: who is?* They can't do shit about anything, anyway. Only people who want to bitch go on the site. So, whatever."

"And you know not to throw vibrators in the washing machine?"

"Of course you don't. It says right on the box." There I go again, spewing at the mouth. From his laugher, he wanted to out me on my vibrator usage. Damn, I shouldn't be insecure about it.

"Good to know," he says, dropping it, but he already got his unspoken answers. "That's damn funny. I'm not sure I can top that one."

"That's only one of them."

"Hell, how many women use your laundromat for their dildos?" His puzzling tone tells me he is really curious.

"A lot. And condoms plugging up the toilet and adhered to the dryer drum. Caught a couple on camera going at it on one of the folding tables. I was wondering why it looked so wobbly and found out quickly why when I checked out the cameras."

"Sounds like someone had some fun."

"I guess. I'm just glad the cleaning service comes in and does their thing. Lord knows what I could catch. Ew ..." Fuck, did I just say that? I seriously just said that ... to Cooper. Fucking hell. There goes my damn mouth. Anything I say is going to make it worse. *I don't have any diseases. I mean, I haven't touched any pussy juice.* I mean, come on. Lose. Lose all the way around.

I love hearing his chuckle, though. At least someone in the world finds me funny. Even if it's over stupid stories.

"Good to know."

Something's been on my mind since one of our first texts. It was about his story when we talked about my mother. I kind of feel like a douche asking, but it's better than doing it over texting.

"Want to tell me what you meant by reminding you to tell me your story later?"

He lets out a long puff of air. "No, not really."

I immediately feel let down. I opened up to him more than I have anyone in a long time. The fact he won't open to me sucks.

"But I will," he finishes, and I let out my own breath. Thank you, God. "My mom is Princess. She's not my biological mom, though. You can't tell anyone this. I'm trusting you with something I don't tell people."

Wow. That's a huge gift he's giving me, and I refuse to take it lightly.

"Mums the word."

"Alright." He blows out a gust of air, and it feels like a heavy weight the way he pauses.

My mind instantly goes to protection mode. It's not something that can be controlled. Whatever he's going to tell me should be done in person or something other than a phone call like this.

"Cooper," I interrupt.

"Yeah?"

"I'm honored that you want to tell me this, but it's heavy, and I really don't think we should do it over the phone." I pause, feeling like an idiot. Here is this man, about to open up to me, and I'm shutting him down. Nevertheless, I have this urge to protect him, which makes it semi-okay ... I think. "It's not that I don't want to know, because I do. I seem to want to know everything about you, but over the phone just doesn't feel right."

I wish I could see him and read his body language. Is he shocked I stopped him? Is he pissed? Does he want to hang up on me and never talk to me again? Or does he respect that I'm trying to keep his secrets as private as possible?

Getting up from my bed, I pace the room and gnaw on my thumbnail when he says nothing. Just dead air over the phone. Shit, I already screwed this up. We should have kept to texting. Then I wouldn't have inserted my foot in my mouth. Dammit.

"I respect that, Bristyl. Thank you."

"You're not pissed at me?"

It sounds as if he's moving on the other end of the phone with the static, maybe getting up or walking somewhere. I'm not sure which.

"Not at all. It's smart. I like the way you think."

I drop to the floor, back against my bed, pulling stray hairs from my face, relief filling me. "Thanks."

"So, tell me, Bristyl, you work at the laundromat and a storage unit. What else do you do? College? Out partying at rallies? Clubbing?"

"Clubbing? Are you serious?" Clubbing? This man ... I shake my head.

"Hell if I know what you chicks do."

Chicks. Well, at least it's better than some of the other terms I've heard over the years.

"What this chick does is work. I didn't do college. Well, I take that back. I did try out of high school, but realized quickly it wasn't for me."

"Why's that? You seem like a really smart girl."

I stare up at the ceiling. "Thanks. I did okay, but doing school on top of work just didn't pan out well."

"So, you hated it?"

I chuckle. "Yeah, pretty much."

"College was never a goal for me. I was born Ravage. I'll die Ravage. That's always been the plan."

That pit of unease creeps back. How soon I keep forgetting that he's in a club and probably feels the same way my father and brothers do. I hate to even think it, but the idea of it rides me hard. Why does he have to be the one that I want to talk to.

I try to push the insecurities down.

"Your brother and sister, are they younger? I'm assuming yes because you called them kids earlier." Way to change the subject, Bristyl.

"Yep. They're fourteen."

"Do you get along with them?"

"For the most part. There's such a huge age gap that it's different. It's like, maybe I'm their cousin or something instead of their brother. But we roll with it."

Our conversation lasts throughout the night, and I fall asleep, still clutching my phone and onto a small bit of hope. Hope that maybe Cooper is different.

CHAPTER TWELVE
Cooper

"What the fuck are you doin' in your room every night? You've bailed on us," Ryker accuses from the passenger seat of the small box truck. We just dropped off a shipment to a client and are on our way back to Ravage.

"Yeah, you wackin' off in there? Because, you're not tappin' anything at the club," Jacks joins in, and he's not wrong.

Something's fucking with my head. No, not something—someone. But I can't seem to stop myself. I look forward to talking to her. It lightens my day and makes anything that's annoying or frustrating disappear. I can talk to her about anything. Feel like shit, then talk to her, and *bam*, feel good.

"I've got shit to do." Keeping my eyes focused on the road, I'm not sure why I don't want to tell them about Bristyl. Maybe it has something to do with having one thing that's solely mine. It's not like she's a forbidden secret or any of that shit. Talking with Bristyl is just different, and I don't know how to explain it to them. They wouldn't get it. At least, I don't think they would.

"Coop, seriously, it's been over a week," Green adds his two cents.

"Have I neglected any of my club responsibilities?" I charge back, feeling fire in my veins. They say nothing, because I haven't. "Anything at the shop or X I haven't done?" Again nothing. I may be talking to

Bristyl, but that doesn't mean I fell down on my job in any way, shape, or form.

"Brother, it's just not you, and we want to know if we can help," Green says, concern in his tone.

"There's nothin' wrong. I appreciate it, but it's all good." I'm not changing what I'm doing. I'm a grown-ass man, and if I want to talk to a woman on the phone and get a few laughs, then I will. What would be better is if I could see her.

Later that night, I call. She answers on the second ring.

"You're early." That damn purr to her voice, and I know she's not even trying. It's all the damn time. Everything she says has it. Hell, she could be talking about something serious or her family and it's there. Makes me so damn rock hard.

"I've got an idea. Saturday, want to meet me in Marianna? That's about an hour drive for you. I'll find a place for us to eat and see each other." Once the thought came into my head in the truck, I couldn't shake it. Seeing her became high on my to-do list.

She doesn't say anything for a few minutes. I'm pretty sure she's shocked.

"How long of a drive is that for you?"

"You don't have to be concerned about that, just think about your drive."

"I damn well have concerns, Cooper. I don't want you driving what? Four, five hours here. I mean ..." She gives a little cough. Her concern for me is cute. "I want to see you. I just don't want anything to happen to you on the road."

A shit-eating grin crosses my face. "That ride's a drop in the bucket. Can you do it?"

"Of course, but—"

"No buts. I don't have shit going on here at the club this weekend. It's perfect timing. And beautiful, it's around three hours. That's really nothin'."

"You sure you want to meet up? Do you think that'll change things?"

"What do you mean *change things?*"

"I don't know. I just feel like I know you, and we've seen each other twice. Doesn't that seem strange to you?"

I chuckle. "Beautiful, everything about this is strange to me. I'm rollin' with it and askin' you to do the same."

"Okay, it's a plan."

"It's a plan."

I roll out early, only stopping when I need to fill up my tank and take a leak. The anticipation of seeing her builds with each passing mile.

As I pull up to the diner, her Dodge Challenger is parked on the right side of the lot. I pull up next to her and shut down my bike. Her sexy blue eyes stare up at me through her window. Damn, she's even better looking than I remembered, or is it actually knowing a woman that makes them more than you envisioned?

I drop the kickstand as she gets out of the car. Bristyl pulls her light blue T-shirt down nervously, her hand giving a slight tremor. There she goes again, being cute.

"Hey, beautiful."

A rosy pigment comes to her cheeks and spreads down her chest. The cut out V doesn't hide anything. Her plump breasts look full pressed against the shirt. I swallow back the saliva that coats my mouth.

"Hey, how was the drive?"

"Good." I slide my glasses off and hook them on my shirt, not wanting any deterrents from seeing Bristyl fully.

"I feel bad you had to drive so far."

"I'm the one who suggested this, remember?" What I don't tell her is I would have driven all the way down if I needed to.

The urge to wrap her in my arms becomes overwhelming, and I give in to it, pulling her to me and pressing her head against my chest. She wraps her arms around my waist and latches her hands together behind my back. When she lets out a deep sigh, I rest my cheek on top of her head. Contentment fills me for the first time ever.

I inhale her branding, her flowery smell, into my memory and enjoy this moment.

After a hard squeeze, I pull back, looking down at her. Her blue eyes sparkle in the sunlight, almost like they're dancing. Bristyl licks her plump bottom lip, and as much as I tell myself to hold back, that I won't take it too far this time, I can't help myself. The need and desire are too much.

Our lips connect as she brings her hands to the front of my T-shirt and grips it tight. She doesn't protest, but it takes her a moment to kiss me back. Once she does, fire, flames, and ignition take over. I can't get enough of her.

She opens her mouth, and I take that as my invitation, sliding my tongue inside, tasting her, savoring her. My dick jumps to attention, and as our bodies touch, I have no doubt she feels it from her shivers. She doesn't blink, though. No, she continues to give as good as she's getting. Then she heaves for breath, and as much as it pains me, I pull back, allowing her to get oxygen into her body. With my forehead on hers, I suck in my own gulps.

That's it. In my gut, I knew at the rally that if I took a taste of her, that would be it. Called it.

Her sweetness is an aphrodisiac that I want more and more of. Her eyes looking at me like I just gave her the world, when it was only one kiss, is it. I feel it inside my chest, and I won't deny it.

Fuck it. She may be too good for my world, but fuck it. She has no idea what she's opened up. It's too late now.

"Wow." She clutches my shirt tighter like she wants to hold on to me for a bit longer. I feel the same, but only my arms are around her body. "That was quite a hello."

"Yeah, beautiful. I've been waiting a damn long time for that."

"Me, too," she whispers. Then she gets up on her tiptoes and places a soft kiss on my lips. "Let's go eat."

Eating is the last thing on my mind, but that's what we came for. To eat and talk, and we'll do it even if it kills me.

I grip her hand as she moves around me to walk into the diner, then lace our fingers together. Her skin is soft, warm, and damn perfect.

I lift our connected hands and kiss the top of hers. Her soft smile hits me deep.

Holding hands, we walk to the building that has a small sign that reads: *The Café*. When I looked it up, it boasts about being a mom and pop shop. Judging from the yellow concrete blocks on the outside and windows with curtains, I can say that's right. The doors to the place are over on each side instead of the front. Going in, I hold the door for Bristyl and let her go in front of me.

"Sit anywhere," a waitress calls out.

The place is definitely a throwback to the sixties or seventies. A light green color vinyl covers the booths with a flower pattern on the back. Wallpaper with the same flowers cover the walls, as well. There's a bar area where one person sits eating. We find a seat away from everyone and climb in, which forces me to let go of her hand so she can slide into the booth.

An older waitress comes to the table wearing tan pants, a white shirt, and a green apron. She hands us a menu that's just a laminated sheet of paper with writing on both sides.

"What can I get y'all to drink?"

I look at Bristyl and wait for her answer.

"Diet Coke please."

"And you?"

"Coke's fine."

"Got it. Be back in a few."

Bristyl picks up her menu and begins to read it. Me, I watch her every movement. She almost feels like a mirage, like if I blink or move wrong, she'll disappear. After lying in bed for so many nights, talking and thinking about her, this seems surreal.

"What's wrong?" she asks, looking up at me.

"Not a damn thing." I leave out how, for the first time in my life, shit feels right.

"Why are you looking at me like that?"

"It's just nice to see you and not just hear your sexy as hell voice."

"My voice isn't sexy."

"Yeah, beautiful, it is."

That shy blush tinges her cheeks again.

"You hungry?" I ask.

"Not really."

This surprises me. "You're not?"

"No, I'm nervous, Cooper. This is so out of my comfort zone it's in another realm."

I reach over and grab her hands. They are ice cold, so I rub them with mine to help warm them, smiling the entire time.

"Out of yours? Try out of mine." She has no clue how far out this is. Take a woman to bed, hell yeah. Actually talk to her every damn night on the phone, drive three plus hours to see her, and sit in some little rinky-dink diner just to spend time with her. Never happened before, but I'm happy to do it with her.

"I'm not sure what we're doing here."

"What can I get ya?" the waitress says, coming back to the table.

Bristyl tries pulling her hands out of my grasp, but I hold tighter, not allowing her to. She doesn't resist.

"Order."

She does, and then I do, thankful when the waitress goes away.

"Let's just see. I can't give you any guarantees. I know I like talking to you every night. I know I like seeing you face to face. I know you make me smile in a way I don't normally." I give her hands a squeeze.

Two hours later, she's laughing so hard tears roll down her face, and we've finished our hundredth glass of soda. The sun is getting low in the sky. With Bristyl having an hour drive, if she leaves now, then she won't have to drive in the dark.

"We should head out."

She says nothing, but the playful smile leaves her face as sadness rolls in. Damn, I didn't realize how much it would suck ass to leave her and drive back home. It's like leaving a piece of yourself behind when all you want to do is throw it on the back of your bike and ride away with it.

I toss down some bills, slide my wallet into my pocket, and reach out for her hand, holding it all the way out the door and to our vehicles. With our hands locked tight, a strange feeling comes over me. A connection so tight the pull to her nearly knocks me on my ass.

Women have always just come and gone. This feeling, though, I want it to stay. It's more than fucking this woman. Everything is real— a bond, a friendship.

When her eyes lift to mine, a slight sheen covering them, I know she feels this, too. This upcoming loss.

I reach around the back of her head and pull her toward me, wrapping her in my warmth. I can't tell her it will be alright, because I have no idea what lies ahead in the future. What I do know is this moment, saying goodbye, doesn't sit right with me.

My lips touch the top of her head, and I feel her shiver.

"I want you to call me when you get home. I probably won't be able to answer, but leave me a message, and I'll call you when I get back to my place."

She nods, her head brushing against my chest.

When I pull back and she looks up, there isn't a single tear cascading down her face, which I'm thankful for. Though, they are in her eyes, ready to fall. She looks as if she's controlling it, and I appreciate that. I don't want my last vision of her to have tears running down her cheeks.

Pressing my lips to hers, they dance slow and steady, savoring each touch, lick, and nibble. The deeper the kiss goes, the stronger I'm pulled to her like a connection that's palpable in so many ways. How this little woman can do this to me is beyond my comprehension.

An invisible string ties itself around me. The pull, the attraction, is too much. Therefore, I stop before it becomes more.

It's not that I don't want to be buried inside her—that's always on my mind. It's that Bristyl isn't a fuck or someone I want to leave the moment we're done. No, I want to hold her, fall asleep with her, and find out what it's like to wake up with a woman I care about beside me. Each of those actions is so foreign, yet feels so right … with her.

"You'd better go," I tell her reluctantly.

"I don't think I want to." She licks her lips, her hands coming to the front of my T-shirt and gripping me tightly. "Say this won't be the last time I see you. Say that we'll meet each other again. Maybe in a different life or something. Just don't say this is the end when I feel like it's just the beginning."

Instead of saying anything, I lean down and take her mouth once more, giving her the words she does and doesn't want to hear from me. When I pull away, I open her car door for her, and she gets in.

"Bye, Cooper," she says on a huff of breath before I close the door, and she drives off like a bat out of hell. Little does she know, she took a piece of me with her.

CHAPTER THIRTEEN

Bristyl

There's no use stopping the tears falling from my eyes. In my gut, I knew it was a bad idea to see him because of this simple reason. When his lips touched mine, I was lost in a way I never wanted to be found again. What was bliss for a few hours is now heartbreak for many more.

The drive is uneventful. The music doesn't help with the feeling of loss inside of me. After getting into my house and locking the door, I text Cooper.

Made it.

I don't hear anything back from him until the morning, when I get: *Home.*

I called him this morning, but it went to voicemail. The pit of loss hit me because he has never let it go to voicemail without telling me he wouldn't be available. I shouldn't have any fears, but maybe it's over. Maybe seeing me that once is enough for him and he's done. Or maybe I'm being an idiot.

"Hey! Where have you been? I've, like, called you a billion times," Leah says from my doorway as I step to the side and let her in. She has called me several times, but I didn't want to hear for the billionth time how sorry she is.

"I've been busy."

"Busy doing what? Besides working."

I wring my hands and wonder if I should tell her about seeing Cooper. Trusting her isn't the problem. It's just nice to have something that's truly mine. Not my father's or brothers or the club's, but mine. It's not that I want him to be a secret, but I guess I do in a way. It's like, if my life is unknown, it won't taint what Cooper and I have together. Damn, I'm confusing.

I wave my hand dismissively. "Just work."

"Yeah. Sorry about ..." she starts, but I hold my hand up to stop her.

"No more, Leah. Stop with this shit. As long as he's not in your business, then don't worry about it. Stop apologizing, because it's bugging the ever-loving shit out of me."

She sighs deeply and falls onto my couch. I sit next to her.

"I know. It just sucks that I was that stupid. But never again."

"Good."

She sighs, and I can tell she just wants things to be normal again.

"So ... I was listening to this radio show this morning, and you're never going to believe this." She turns toward me excitedly, and I try to give it back to her, but I'm sure I fail miserably. It sucks, because my best friend is here, yet my head is hundreds of miles away, wondering why Cooper didn't answer his phone.

"This radio show has people call in for these second chance date things. Like, they go on a date with someone and then the other person doesn't call them back and they want to know why. Now, why someone would actually do this is totally beyond me because—hello—you already went there once and got burned. Now you want to know why and go on another date with them?"

I just smile and let her continue.

"Okay, so this guy Dave calls in. He went on a date with Stacy to a club where they danced and had a good time. While they were dancing, another guy came up and cut in on Stacy. Dave stepped back and let this happen, going to the bar and drinking. Stacy comes back, and they have an okay time, but Dave feels Stacy is off. Stacy tells Dave at the end of the date that she will be gone for two months and won't be able to be reached. I mean, hello, man, red flag! Well, Dave thinks that Stacy doesn't want to go out with him again because he didn't defend her honor by telling the guy to fuck off when he cut in."

"I can see that." My brothers wouldn't allow that to happen one bit. I can see them kicking some serious ass for anyone attempting to cut in when they have a woman, or hell, even cut them in line somewhere.

"Okay, so this radio show calls Stacy, and she literally groans when she hears Dave's name and does the whole, *I'm not going to talk about it on the radio show* thing. Which, who can blame her, putting all her shit out there like that? Anyway, the radio guys tell her why Dave thinks she hasn't called him. She bursts out laughing, saying that it's the total opposite. The radio guys are like *what?* all questioning and stuff. So, Stacy then proceeds to say that, after she got done with her dance with random dude, Dave pulled her over into the corner of the bar and started whispering in her ear."

"That's never a good sign," I say on a chuckle.

"No. Get this. He wanted her to lure the dancing guy outside so he could show him his karate moves. Like, legit. Dave even demonstrated in the bar with his hands how he would break the guy's neck."

"Oh, my God, just for dancing he's going to kill him? Guy sounds like a nut." My brothers would totally kick someone's ass for this, but never kill them for it. At least, I don't think so.

"I know, right? Well, the radio people are laughing hysterically, and Dave comes on the line. He then proceeds to tell Stacy that he had to defend her honor, and the only way to do that was to end this man for disrespecting him."

"Wow."

"I mean, I'm all for a guy sticking up for me and all, but this Dave guy went into it, talking about how he's a master in karate and knows how to defend her. That he'll protect her by any means necessary. On and on. Now, maybe if they'd been dating a while and they, like, love each other, I can see a man standing up like that, but this is their first date!"

I laugh hysterically, my stomach clenching and unclenching as I double over. "Holy shit, that's funny as hell."

"Yeah. Thank God that wasn't us."

"No shit. Wanna go shopping? I need a new bag."

Leah rolls her eyes. "You don't need a new bag; you just want one."

"True."

Women have all different obsessions when it comes to clothes and accessories. Mine are handbags. I love them. They don't have to be the expensive, you-must-give-me-your-first-born-child ones. Nope. Some of the best ones I found are from discount retail stores. I don't care about the name on the purse, or if it's some great fashion designer that I've never heard of. Nope. I only care about how it feels when I carry it, and if I can put all my shit in it.

A day shopping with my best friend will keep me from checking my phone every few minutes, which I'm catching myself doing.

When it does ring, I'm looking at a blue bag that's the color of Cooper's eyes, and excitement courses through me. I hold up a finger to Leah and step away to the side.

"Hello?"

"Hey, beautiful." His sexy as hell voice comes over the line, shaking me to my core.

No one can wipe the ear-to-ear grin from my face. How can two simple words make me feel so damn happy? Him calling me beautiful without even blinking is the best feeling in the world, besides being in his arms.

"Did you get some sleep?"

"Yeah, just rollin' out of bed."

I smirk. "Must be nice. Not all of us get to sleep the day away."

"It's a hard job, but somebody's gotta do it."

I look around, seeing Leah staring at me knowingly. I turn my back to her.

"I'm out shopping with Leah; can I call you back later?"

"Sure thing. Later."

"Later." I swipe the phone off and clutch it to my chest.

"You got a man," Leah says from behind me, making me jump out of my skin.

"Don't do that!"

"What? Come up behind you? Or tell you something you already know?"

"I'm not talking about it right now." I move past her, grabbing the bag I was looking at and then setting it back down. I'm really over shopping right now, especially now that Leah has a bone and won't let up.

"You have a guy, and you're keeping him from me?" Her hands fly to her hips in bitch stance, and other people in the store start looking at us. Great.

"Later." I skate around her and through the store toward the exit, Leah hot on my heels, blathering on.

Once we get in the car, I turn toward her. "Look, everything is new. It may not go anywhere, and you know how my brothers and father are. I just want to keep it to myself until I figure out if it's something or nothing."

Her eyes narrow as if she's delving into the recesses of my brain and picking it apart. We've been friends for too long; she'll get it. If not right now, she will in a couple of days.

"Please just let it go."

Surprisingly, she drops it, but out of the corner of my eye, I see her festering and planning. Damn.

I can't believe I'm doing this again. After the pain from last time, it still doesn't stop me from driving the hour or so to meet Cooper the next Saturday in Cottondale.

I stop at the restaurant and see him sitting on his bike, waiting for me. His nice ass is resting on the seat while his legs are extended out, crossed at the ankles. Damn, he's hot. He's wearing those mirrored shades that look so gorgeous on him, like they were made specifically for him. His jeans fit him perfectly, along with his T-shirt and leather. His long hair glistens in the slight breeze. He is a concoction that dampens panties around the world.

And he's here for me.

I stop the car, turn off the engine, and before my hand touches the door handle, he's there to do it for me. I rise out of the car, feeling his body heat from a few feet away, craving that close connection.

Talking on the phone, learning about each other in a way that's so new to me, having him this close is overwhelming as so many emotions filter through my body. Each one of those—the fear, the lust, the attraction—leads me to the conclusion that I want to see more of Cooper.

Wishing upon a star has never been my thing, but I may have to give it a shot.

"Hi." Why is it that I feel stupid with that one little word? If something cooler would come to mind, that would be great.

He says nothing, just wraps his arms around me, pulling me flush to his body. Then his lips attack mine, and I'm lost. Lost in him. Lost in the moment. Just lost. Everything in my brain stops, and my only focus is the man in front of me.

This goes on for long moments, and I suck each one like a starving woman. When Cooper pulls away on a chuckle, I catch myself leaning into him, trying to follow his lips. How embarrassing, but I don't care.

He reaches over and grabs a helmet. "Put this on."

"You know that Florida doesn't have a law on helmets," I tell him.

He quirks his brow. "And you know this how?"

"Just the guys around here don't wear one often."

"In Georgia, it's law. You on my bike is law. Precious cargo," he says with that sexy smile while my heart warms.

I put it on without any retorts. After all, I'm *precious cargo*.

It's not my first time on a bike, but it will be my first time on a bike with a hot guy that I'm not related to.

He moves to straddle the steel machine. "Get on."

I swing my leg over, thankful I have my chucks on and not flip flops. Cooper pulls my arms around him, and I hold on tight as he takes off like a shot. Having him so close to my body and the rumble of the bike wakes my girly bits up from a way too long nap.

I want to ask him how he can ride again already after he rode such a long time here, but I can't because of the wind in our faces. Instead, I hang on tight and enjoy the ride, letting the cool breeze wash away everything but him and me.

Riding with a man is so much different than with my father or brothers. With Cooper, it's an erotic feeling. The way the bike glides and turns, our bodies following. The way the curve of his back fits perfectly against my front, pressing into my breasts. Everything is so much better being on the back of his bike.

Riding with Sinisters, I always craved to belong. Riding with Coop, I just do. There's no trying involved.

Cooper pulls back into the restaurant we originally came to and comes to a stop. While I loved being on his bike, it's been a while and my legs feel a little jellied when I get off. He reaches out and steadies me, though, and once I have my shit together, he lets go, but laces his fingers with mine.

"Let me feed you."

I can think of a lot of things I want to eat right now, but food isn't one of them. Everything I want revolves around this man in front of me as he leads me into the very brightly lit place. Windows line the walls and florescent lights glare everywhere. This place is definitely not as cozy as the place before, but it is what it is. All I care about is spending time with Cooper.

Cooper finds us a spot in the back, sitting with his back to the wall. He does the exact same thing my father and brothers do. I've been told they have to have eyes on the room at all times.

"Like to sit by the wall?" I tease.

"Nah, I just like to know what's goin' on." He reaches over and grabs my hands. "You're welcome to come over here and sit with me."

My body screams *yes!* but I stay where I am, knowing if I'm sitting that close to him, I won't be able to not touch him. He's too delicious not to, and after that kiss earlier, I want more. So much more. My body craves him with a need so deep it presses against my soul.

A flirty waitress comes and takes our order. Before I know it, the food is in front of us, and I'm sad this is almost over. A few hours isn't enough time. Even eating slow and having a great conversation isn't long enough. It's just not. It royally sucks.

Cooper pays the check, and then we walk solemnly out to my car and his bike where he turns me and presses my body against the car, attacking me with his lips in the most delectable way.

I pull away abruptly. "Stay with me tonight. Don't go back. We can find a place, just you and me, and leave first thing in the morning."

He rocks back on his boots, hands still touching me. For a moment, I can't believe those words just came from my lips, but I want it badly. From his expression, he doesn't, which baffles me. He is a red-blooded male, and the way his lips attacked mine … He has to want this, too, right?

"I'm sorry. I shouldn't have asked that. I need to get going." I try to move away, feeling so damn stupid for even suggesting it. The foot in mouth syndrome hits yet again. I really should stick to text messages or just avoid people altogether.

His grip gets tighter on my hips, stilling me. When I look into his eyes, they burn with an intensity that he's kept from me in our brief encounters. Something devilish and intriguing that makes my knees weak.

"Bristyl, if we go someplace private, I can't guarantee I'll keep my hands off you. It's fuckin' killin' me to leave you as it is."

"What if I don't want you to keep your hands off?" I rise up on my tiptoes and place a soft kiss against his mouth. "I want this, Cooper. Do you?"

"Hell yeah." He crashes his lips back down on mine and takes my breath away. Excitement and anticipation flood my system. "Follow close."

He hops on his bike, and I get in my car. I can't believe I'm doing this, but it's Cooper. The guy who stays up with me all night, talking about stupid shit he shouldn't care about. I want this with him.

I have nothing with me, which makes it all the more exciting. This impulsiveness to take what I want and not sit around, just thinking about it over and over like a movie reel.

We stop at a hotel I didn't see on the way. Cooper gets off his bike and waves for me to stay inside the car.

Once he comes out of the office, I open the door and follow him. It's a nice place. One of those hotel chains you see everywhere and on television.

Cooper closes the door to the room, his focus on me. It makes me feel sexy and desirable, something I haven't really felt before. Sex has always been a means to an end for me. Especially with my brothers acting the way they do. This feels different. It feels real, honest, caring.

Then I remember. "I need to use the bathroom."

His lip rise. He better not say I'm cute. I just need to freshen up. Hell, I was on a bike for hours and need to make sure everything is good.

He says nothing, so I slip into the all-white bathroom that holds the normal things—tub, sink, toilet. Lifting my arms, I smell myself. The deodorant is holding its own. Then I go pee and check everything down there. How embarrassing would it be if I sweat or something down there? Oh God.

After a quick clean up with a damp washrag, I flush, wash, look at myself in the mirror, and jump back. My hair is everywhere. I didn't even think to put it back before the ride, and this is the thanks I get for that one.

Running my fingers through the knots, it takes a while before I see the light at the end of the tunnel. My face is just going to have to work. No zits, so that's a good thing.

I'm such a dork. Only I would run into the bathroom when a hot guy looks at me like I'm his meal and worry about sweat. I'd bang my head against the door, but then he'd hear how big of a fool I am.

Sucking in a deep breath, I open the door. The sight before me is compelling. Cooper is lying back on the bed, T-shirt and jeans on, boots and socks off, arms locked behind his head, looking as cool as a cucumber. Or, I should say, as hot as the desert. My mouth suddenly feels really dry.

"Come here, beautiful." He taps the bed next to him in invitation.

I kick off my shoes and climb in. He positions me so my head is on his chest and arm around my body before he strokes my hair. I'm thankful I took the few minutes to get the knots out of it.

His heart thumps in my ear at a rhythmic pace, calming me. This isn't what I planned, but it's nice. Relaxing almost to the point my eyes want to droop. Who knew he'd be such a great, warm pillow?

I lift my head and rest my chin on his chest, not wanting to fall asleep and miss a moment of our time together. "Are you tired?"

He pulls me completely on top of him, taking all my weight. "No."

Cooper kisses me, moving his hand around the back of my head and filtering his fingers through my hair. That one move is so damn sexy it spikes my arousal into overdrive. My legs spread wide, straddling him, while he brings his other hand to the side of my face.

"The whole way here, I kept tellin' myself I need to go slow." This declaration shocks me. "Can't, beautiful. I've had a raging hard-on since I saw you in that laundromat. There's no waiting and no being gentle."

My heart thumps hard as it pumps blood throughout my body.

"I just want you," I whisper as he presses his lips to mine.

CHAPTER FOURTEEN

Cooper

Going slow isn't an option. I thought I could pull it off, but I was kidding myself. I have wanted this woman for weeks now. She's all I think about, dream about, and long to talk to. She has a beauty that is unprecedented. Combined with her quirkiness and the way she makes me laugh, she's an intoxicating woman.

I flip her so she lies beneath me, and she moves her hands to the back of my shirt, sliding under the fabric. My body trembles at the contact.

She's never looked more beautiful than this moment, splayed beneath me with desire bright in her eyes. Lucky doesn't even cut it. The fact that I'm here and not some other schmuck is a godsend. She's too damn good to be true, but feeling her beneath me, she is.

When I trail kisses down her jaw and neck, Bristyl's hips grind up into me, only making my already painfully hard cock jump and twitch to get out. Then I reach down and pull her T-shirt up, exposing just a patch of skin, then more and more, until it's off her body completely. The light pink lace bra is sexy as fuck and makes me wonder if Bristyl is innocent. She seems shy, but not to the point I'd call her a virgin. If she is, I hope she says something.

Reaching behind her, I unclasp the bra and pull it from her plump breasts. The light pink tips of her areolas beg for me. Leaning down and taking a pebbled tip in my mouth, her back bows as she gasps.

With my other hand, I massage her other breast, squeezing and pinching the tip, alternating my mouth on each of them. The softness of her skin makes my dick turn to stone.

She threads her hands through my hair, gripping it tightly. I fucking love that. It's one of my biggest turn-ons.

I move to unbuckle her jean shorts, but she beats me to it, tugging them off roughly and tossing them, along with her panties, to the floor. I fully admit, one hundred and ten percent, I'm a pussy man. I can feast on one for hours and never get enough. With Bristyl's pink lips staring back at me, there is nothing stopping me.

Her taste explodes on my tongue, sweet and tangy, a drug. Yes, one taste, and it should be classified as an illegal substance to everyone, but me.

"Oh, Cooper!" she yells, her hands back in my hair as I grip her thighs and eat—licking, nipping, and sucking.

Her nub calls to me, and I wrap my lips around the hard flesh, sucking hard as she screams and explodes on my face. I don't stop, not even when her hips buck so hard it threatens to knock me back. Working her down, I then lift my head to watch her pant for breaths, her eyes closed with ecstasy written all over her. Fucking beautiful.

Standing up, I strip and grab the condom out of my wallet. It's the only one I have, which really sucks, but now is not the time to focus on that.

I put it on quickly before climbing back on the bed and pulling her up to straddle me, her eyes flashing open.

"I want you to ride me. Show me what my bike did for you."

A sexy as hell smirk spreads across her lips. "You sure you want that," she teases, tracing my pec with her finger, and then down my abs.

"Fuck yeah."

"You asked for it." She lifts then ever so slowly wraps her warmth around my cock, squeezing the very breath from me. Tight. No, she's a fucking vice. Maybe I should have loosened her up some more so it doesn't hurt.

Somehow, she seats herself all the way on my shaft. I wait for her to say it's painful, yet she doesn't.

"You're so big. I feel you everywhere."

I buck my hips in an aroused response.

She brings her hands to my chest, knees planted on the bed, and she rides. Up and down. Down and up. She circles her hips to the right, then swirls them to the left, and begins this vicious pattern, integrating it with up and down movements. The blaze inside me roars to life. I know for damn sure this isn't her first time, but I shut that thought right down.

I rise up, our chests flushed, and kiss her hard before rolling us over. I can't stop. I don't want to stop. My hips thrust hard over and over, and she meets me at every movement, making it feel so much better.

"Cooper, I'm coming!" she screams.

Her walls contract around me, making the already tight space suffocating. Her pussy sucks the come from my cock, while my legs strain as I push my cock inside her as far as humanly possible, all thoughts of breathing gone. Then we still together.

This connection is life altering. It's everywhere. Her. Me. Us. It's so incredibly strong that it shakes me to my core.

Falling to the side, my cock slips out of her. I scoop her panting body into my arms and hold her as tightly as I possibly can. Nothing in the world exists in this moment. Nothing. Only Bristyl and me. Only this connection we share. I have never felt closer to a person, not ever.

I lightly stroke Bristyl's hair, waiting for her to open her eyes. Once she does, I see something in there shining brightly. I've never had it before, so I don't want to assume anything. Assuming things gets a man killed. Facts, one can survive on.

"That was …" she starts, unable to form words.

I have to agree with her. "Yeah."

Seeing a box of tissues on the nightstand, I remove the condom and toss it to the floor, not wanting to leave her for a minute. Then I pull her tighter to me, grab the comforter, and flip it on us so we are in a cocoon of warmth. It doesn't take long before we fall fast asleep.

Shots are fired in every direction. My mother goes down with a thump as I lay, covering a woman who's bleeding out everywhere. Looking down, Bristyl's lifeless body stares back at me.

I jolt upright, looking around the room. A body flies off me as I take in the space. Hotel. Bristyl. *Shit.*

I flip the light on to see her pulling the hair away from her groggy face, half on the bed, half off.

"What's wrong?"

Grabbing her, I hold her close. She's alive. She's safe. She's here. The relief is so damn overwhelming it threatens to strangle my breaths.

"Just a bad dream."

I allow her warmth to heat me, taking me away from the nightmare. Her touch pulls me away from the fear, which doesn't hit me often. Seeing Bristyl dead … that's a horrible fear.

"Do you have those often?"

"I have them quite a bit." Admitting that is hard. No one knows about them. I've been able to hide them from the guys and women— no woman has ever spent the night beside me to learn of them. Weakness. That's what I tell myself. Having the guys or anyone know about them isn't in the cards. Yet Bristyl knowing feels right.

"Want to tell me about them?"

"No," I answer immediately, not wanting to tell her that I held her lifeless body in my hands inside that cloud. "But I will tell you where they come from."

"I'll listen to whatever you want to tell me."

Inhaling the cool air, we tangle our legs together, bodies flushed. "When I was young, like, really little, a man came into the Ravage clubhouse holding a gun to my grandmother's head. Not only that, he shot my mother. I saw it all, and the woman protecting me had to cover my mouth so I wouldn't scream. My dreams come from that."

"Oh, Cooper."

I shake my head. "I don't want pity; that's not why I told you. I did because I trust you with that information and to keep it right here, between you and me."

"Absolutely. Is your mom and grandma okay?"

I squeeze her a little tighter. "Yeah. They are."

"Good. And you're safe, so that's all that matters." She presses into me, her head on my chest, arms around my body. All I can think is *and so are you.*

"You said that Princess isn't really your mom? I don't understand." Her words are soft and comforting.

I glide my hand up and down her back as the weight of years lays on my shoulders. "Not biologically, but in every other way possible. My incubator, as my mother calls her, was a drug addict. My father told me a few things, but both he and my mom kept a lot from me, saying they didn't want to taint my life with my biological mother's shit. Her name was Mel, and she didn't love me. All the memories I have of her are bad."

"Oh, Cooper." Her grip gets tighter as she tries to pull away to look into my eyes, but I hold her tight. This is hard enough talking about without the weight of her thoughts on me, as well. "I ..."

"It is what it is. I have a great mom and more than I could ask for. Mel was going to give me to a crazy lady, but ended up dead." Her body jolts at that. "I can't tell you all the details because it's club business, but what I can tell you is that my mom saved me in more ways than one."

"I'm so happy you have that."

"Me, too. Who the hell knows how my life would have turned out had Mel been a part of it?"

"Does it bother you that she's dead?"

It surprises me that she didn't ask how she died. I respect that.

"No, not Mel. If it would have been my mom, that would have killed."

"I know what that's like." Her voice goes soft again.

"How long ago did your mom pass?"

She heaves in a breath. "When I was sixteen ... so about five years now. Wow. It feels like it happened yesterday."

"Sorry, beautiful."

"Me, too. She was amazing. It was an aneurism that took her. It happened so fast that we had no warning at all. *Boom*, she was here ... then she was in a casket." Her body shakes, and I hold her tighter.

"She made you, so I bet she was great."

Bristyl pulls away and smiles up at me like I'm the only thing in her world. I want to be that. I crave to be that.

"Yeah." She reaches up and touches her lips to mine then pulls back and a yawn escapes her, along with a giggle.

"Sleep, beautiful. I'm right behind ya." My grip tightens on her as I feel her body relax, falling back asleep.

Dread fills me as I look at the clock. It'll be morning soon, and then I'll have to leave. Again.

That's it. I'm strapping her to my bike, and she's coming with me. On that thought, sleep consumes me.

"Hey," a purr of a voice says above my head.

When I open my eyes, Bristyl is above me, her hair in a ponytail, face beautiful as always, and she's dressed.

"Why are you dressed?"

"I have to go."

Glancing at the clock, I see it's ten-o-nine.

"Shit," I grumble, grabbing her arm and pulling her down to me, kissing her the entire time. Her giggles are squashed by my lips.

As much as I need to go to a family night tonight at the clubhouse and I can't miss it, there's nothing that's going to stop me from having her again.

All the while kissing her, I flip her on her back and unbutton her shorts. Then she wiggles out of them without protest.

The kisses are heated and demanding. Our teeth clash as if we would climb into each other if we could. When my cock strains, it hits me. I don't have a fucking rubber.

"I don't have another condom."

She smiles. "I do." Bristyl reaches down into her bag and pulls one out.

"I'm not gonna think that those were for any asshole but me."

"They weren't. Just bought them." She smiles wickedly.

I take her hard and rough, to the point we are both screaming out our releases. Unfortunately, we then both have to go, so holding her isn't an option.

"You've got a sweet tongue."

"Don't you know it." I wink as I throw my clothes on. Then I use the bathroom, and we are ready to roll.

As we stand at her car, my chest tightens all over again.

"Wanna hop on my bike and come with me?"

"More than you want to know."

"Then do it. Come home with me."

She looks down at the ground. "I'm bound to my family. I can't just leave them like that."

"I want this, Bristyl. I want what we had last night over and over again. I want you in my bed, in Georgia. You want it, too."

She gives a slight nod.

"We need to figure out a way to make that happen."

"You want me to leave everyone I know and move in with you? Don't you think that's going a bit too fast?"

I kiss her breathlessly. "What do you think?"

She shakes her head. "I don't know what to think, Cooper."

"Just think on it. That's all I'm asking."

"Okay."

"Now kiss me."

"I bet you say that to all the girls," she teases, and I love it.

"No, only you."

Our lips collide.

After loading her into the car, seeing the small tears in her eyes, I pack up and head back home, disliking each mile between us. This is going to come to an end sooner rather than later.

"You're late," my mother calls out from the kitchen as I enter the clubhouse.

Even coming right here, I'm late and tired as fuck. With so little sleep last night and the drive, I could pass out for days.

"I'm here. Let that be enough."

I head into my room, splash some cool water on my face, and put on a new shirt. Family time needs to happen fast so I can crash for work tomorrow.

"Cooper!" my sister yells from across the clubhouse, running up and hugging me.

Being fourteen, I'm sure those days are going to be less and less. It would be nice if she stayed this sweet, little girl for as long as humanly possible. Or, at least not turn into a bitch of a teenager.

"How's it goin'?"

"Good. I got an A on my English paper, but a D in math. I don't know how the teachers expect you to know all of this stuff." Her hand goes to her hip as I wrap my arm around her shoulders.

Heading outside, greetings come from all angles, along with shit from the guys for not coming home last night. It all rolls off my back.

The burgers are fantastic, and it's nice to see the kids play on the shit I did a long time ago. Well, it feels like a long time ago.

Thoughts of Bristyl here with me, sitting next to me and talking with my family come to mind. She's never too far from my thoughts. Ever. I hope she realizes how serious I am about her coming here.

Strolling back into the clubhouse, I see Deke sitting at a table by himself, twirling a metal ashtray. He looks up, scoffs, and goes back to his twirling. I sit down in the chair in front of him, but he doesn't say anything.

When we were younger, we were always hanging out together. That all stopped when I got about fifteen, sixteen. He seemed so young then, and I was getting into shit he didn't need to be a part of. We drifted apart.

"What's goin' on?" I pull out my smokes and light one.

"Go away." When he looks up at me, there's a sinister glint in his eye. One I've never seen on him. Come to notice, his eyes are bloodshot, as well.

"Did you take somethin'?"

"Go. The fuck. Away," he growls.

"Answer the question. What did you take?" The erratic behavior, the obvious temper flair, bloodshot eyes, fidgeting. Hell, it could be a number of things.

"You think you're so fuckin' perfect." He stands, or tries to, but wobbles. Yes, he's definitely on something.

I search the room and see Buzz. "Go get GT."

He nods and leaves.

"Oh, yeah, call my daddy. Just so you know, I'm blood," he spits out, pointing to his chest. "I'm real Ravage blood. Two presidents and my dad are Ravage. This will be mine, not yours!" He comes at me, but he's so out of it that I'm able to grab him around his arm and halt him.

"What the fuck are you talkin' about?"

"*Why can't you be more like Cooper? Why can't you act like him? Why don't you treat your sister like he does his? Why don't you get your shit together so you can prospect like Cooper did at sixteen?* Cooper. Cooper. Cooper."

I release him and push him away from me.

He turns. "It's always about you! The fuckin' golden boy, who can never do no wrong, Cooper. Don't think the other kids don't see it, too. We all have to live up to the mighty you. Well, fuck you!"

GT comes in through the doors, pulling his sunglasses off. "What's goin' on?"

"Let me guess. Gonna take me away so I don't embarrass you because Cooper never embarrasses anyone!" Deke screams.

GT looks at me, and I shrug. "Apparently, this is Deke's club because he's blood and I'm not." I shake my head. "He's on somethin', GT. He's not thinkin' clearly. Need to get him some help."

"Help? No, I need to get away from you!"

"That's enough." GT grabs Deke's neck and pulls him out of the clubhouse.

Angel, who stepped in after GT, wipes a tear from her eye.

"Nothin' like a good ol' family quarrel. Now, let's drink!" Ryker calls out.

The shots keep coming, and I keep taking them. One after the other. My girl isn't here, Deke has lost his damn mind, and again, I'm here. My head swims as Tina, one of the club mommas, comes up to me.

"Hey, Coop. Haven't seen you in a while." She traces my arm and goes under the arm hole of my shirt.

The smell of her instantly hits my nostrils, and I jerk my head slightly. It's a floral scent, but not like the kind Bristyl wears. No, this is fake, a cheap imitation, and I want nothing to do with it.

"Been busy," I clip, just wanting her to leave.

"How about we go play?" She traces my arm with a finger, and I automatically bounce back.

I may be drunk, but Tina doesn't hold a candle to Bristyl.

"No. Go find someone else and tell all the others I said no."

"Seriously? You've been gone forever." The damn woman pouts.

Anger fully hits me. "You either get out of my sight and do as you're told, or get the fuck out. You choose."

"Sorry." She steps back and scurries away.

"What crawled up your ass?" Ryker asks, sitting down next to me.

"Tired. I'm callin' it a night."

He looks to his watch. "Dude, it's, like, eleven."

"And?" I walk off, stumbling to my room and locking the door behind me, not listening if Ryker answered my rhetorical question.

My phone rings as I fall into the bed. Pulling it out of my cut, I see it's Bristyl, so I answer.

"Hey, beautiful."

"Hey. You made it home in time?" Her voice is quiet like she's lying in bed.

"Nah, I was late. My mom gave me shit, but there's nothin' new with that."

She chuckles on the other end, and a deep feeling of loss hits my gut. I want her here, in my arms, lying with me, and not hundreds of miles away.

She yawns loudly. "I need sleep, but I wanted to make sure you were there, safe."

I love that she cares for me enough that she had to make sure I was okay. Damn.

"I'm here. Night, beautiful."

"Night."

I click the phone off and pass out.

"So, we have a problem," Pops says, sitting at the head of the table in church. He called the meeting yesterday after a phone call he received from the Red Devils MC. The one that asshole Nick is a part of.

"It seems that Nick has a totally different story on what happened. His president, Scandal, has called a meeting that we need to go down to Florida to handle. I'm not fuckin' happy about this." Pops' eyes come directly at me, boring a hole in my damn head. "Especially since you haven't put claim on this woman. So, we're in a pile of shit because of some bitch you had a hard-on for, and this isn't how shit works." His fist comes down on the table hard, shaking it.

My fists clench tight and anger boils below the surface. I learned to remain calm on the outside, but that doesn't mean I'm not livid with Pops right now. He has no idea what Bristyl means to me.

"She's not some random bitch I fucked in a damn bathroom." My words are low and menacing.

"You haven't even seen her since the rally," my father charges back.

My gaze shoots to him. "That's where you're wrong. I've seen her the past few Saturdays and talk to her every damn night. She is mine."

A surprised look crosses his face. I don't know why, considering I don't tell him every little thing about my life. I am who I am.

"Then why isn't she here?" Rhys asks, stroking his face. "Pick her up and bring her ass here."

"I'm workin' on it."

"Workin' on it or doin' it?" Rhys has always been an intense man. He sees something he wants, he takes it. Me, I've always been a bit more laid back, but that time has come to an end.

"Doin'," I respond, looking at Pops. "Let's meet him."

"We're all goin'. Two days." Pops tosses down the gavel.

Fuck. I need a plan, and I need my woman.

CHAPTER FIFTEEN

Bristyl

He's coming. Excited isn't even the word to describe how I feel inside. I've been busting my ass today, trying to get all caught up so nothing will tie me down. He says he has to work, which is totally fine. I just don't want to be returning phone calls when I could be spending time with Cooper. He said he would spend a couple of extra days down here with me, too. So, no way am I letting work get in the way of that.

To have days of just him and me alone ... My body quivers remembering how he felt inside of me. That one on one, face to face time is what I crave every moment of the day, and now we're going to have it for more than a night.

A knock comes to my office door, and when I look up, Racer is leaning against the doorframe, arms crossed.

"Well, hello, brother," I say, giving a small wave then going back to my papers.

He says nothing as he steps inside the office. The distinct sound of him closing the door has my head popping up. My door doesn't get closed unless it's something serious. I don't want serious right now. The high of having Cooper here is great, and I want to ride the wave.

"What's wrong?" My mind immediately goes to either a brother or my father being hurt, and my chest tightens at the thought.

He takes a seat in front of me, elbows to his knees, eyes on me. "Got shit goin' down." Racer pauses. Racer never hesitates. It's not in his nature. Again, unease washes over me. "I drew the short straw. Bristyl our Pistol, you gotta know this isn't what any of us wanted for you. Time's come, though. Decision is on you, but you gotta pick." He runs his hands through his hair in obvious frustration. "Shit burns me to say, but Bristyl, Sterling, he's stepping up and will claim you. You gotta either take his property patch as an ol' lady, or Bris, you gotta be a whore."

My jaw falls to the floor, picking up every speck of dust possible, and my throat becomes impeccably dry. He didn't just say that to me. Holy fuck, he did. Never in my life would I ever think those words would escape my brother's mouth.

"You want me to become an ol' lady or a ... whore? What's gotten into you?"

"I know Dad's talked to you."

"He's said that I'm not an ol' lady, so I don't have the same rights as the ones here in the club. But he said that I'm an employee of the club. He never said anything about becoming one, let alone someone who sleeps with the entire club." Sickness rolls in my stomach, threatening to expel from my body. That is so not my gig.

"Great, he left that up to me." My brother looks at the ceiling like this is killing him. Well, if only he knew what it's doing to me. "Look, Bristyl, we have club rules here. You being our sister gives us some leeway on protecting you, but it would be better if you were a part of the club so we can really enforce that. We've pushed as hard as we can, but we're gettin' some flak for it because no one else gets what you get from the club. Shit's gettin' deeper than ever before for the club. Dad, Stone, Hunter, and me, we need to know you're protected. Sinisters can do that and will do that, but only if you take it on your back or the back of a brother's bike for life."

"So, you're saying that I'm in danger and if I don't buddy up with someone, I'm going to be hurt."

He leans back in the chair, casual as can be. "You have two options in this club. Ol' lady or a club whore. There is no in between. Both we protect, each at different levels. You being the sister is lower on that totem pole. So, if you became an ol' lady, we could work with this better."

"You've got to be shitting me." I realize I'm holding a pen in my hand and toss it on the stack of papers in frustration. "I'm not going to be either. One, I'm not spreading my legs for guys here to take their turn with me. That doesn't fly with me. Some women it does, and good for them, but not me. Second, there is no way I'll be Sterling's ol' lady. He doesn't even like me, just wants me on his arm. How can you even ask this of me?"

"No one said you had to like the guy. Just keep him happy. Then we have the clout with the club to keep you under protection."

"So, in turn, fuck him so I'm protected? This is absolutely the stupidest thing I've ever heard. I can't believe you're sitting there, saying this to me. I don't want to be an ol' lady in Sinisters."

He shrugs. "Then you become a whore. At least you know four of us who won't touch you."

My stomach curls again. "No, I'm not."

He rises from his chair and stretches so damn nonchalantly that it pisses me off. It's like he doesn't realize he just flipped my world upside down.

This isn't happening. I've been bound to my family for years, but them asking this of me ... No, it's not happening.

Racer opens the door. "Think about it. We want an answer next week. Got shit to do." Then he leaves. Gone. Poof. Like a cloud of smoke.

I'm pissed as hell and hurt. How can my own brother, my own family, want to pimp me out to his friends? Either way, that's what this is. It's either one or all of them. How can a man I've known all my life suggest this to me, let alone expect an answer by next week? He's lost his mind. This has got to be a cruel joke.

I march from my office and search for my father, finding him in the back room, talking with Wolf. The hesitation is only a second, but I knock as his eyes lift.

"Can I talk to you?"

"In a minute. I'll be in your office. Close the door," he dismisses me while Wolf gives me a look that has me darting from the door.

All those old feelings of when I was younger come rushing back. I'm not good enough unless I'm what they want me to be.

Sitting in my chair, my leg bobs up and down, never stopping. My nerves are going haywire.

My father comes in casually and sits in the same chair my brother just vacated.

"Racer just came in here saying I need to become and ol' lady or a whore. What's that about?"

He blows out a breath, the hairs on his mustache blowing with it. "Our club rules. You're my daughter, so you've gotten leeway, but you're twenty-one now and that's runnin' out. You either need to be in the club or you're out. I want you in so I can keep you safe."

"Do you hear what you're saying right now?"

"Yes, and it's how it is." He's stoic.

I can't help wondering what it would take to break my father. He really can't think this is my only option.

This sudden turn is crippling me. This is not the man that I know.

"I can't believe you'd want me to be unhappy just to cover your rules." Pain engulfs me.

I wish my mother was still alive. There's no way she would allow this.

He leans forward as darkness covers his eyes. It has me sitting back in my chair.

"That's how this shit works. You don't like the rules, then you leave."

"Are you firing me?"

"If I have to." My father has never talked to me like this in my whole damn life. Surely this isn't the man that my mother loved, or maybe this is the side I've never known. "I'm doing what I know to do to keep you in the fold. You don't want that, I can't make you stay. But I can't change the situation, either."

"I don't even know what to say."

He shrugs, and it hurts. The nonchalance is more than hurting me, it's searing pain. I can't see why this is even an option.

I look for some sign on him. The wrinkles around his eyes or lips to see if something is wrong, but he remains his cool and calm self.

"It's you're in or out. If you're out, you're all the way out. It's time. We'll need an answer next week." He gets up and leaves my office as tears well up in my eyes.

This can't be happening. It just can't.

Cooper is the first person who comes to mind. I need him to hold me right now and warm me from the chill I just got from the people I thought would love me until I died. However, this isn't something I can tell him over the phone. He will be here tomorrow. I just need to hold myself together until then.

"What's wrong?" How Cooper got that from me telling him hello, I'll never know. It doesn't bode well if he can tell my emotions just by words over a phone hundreds of miles away.

"Just a long day." I refuse to lie to him, but what I have to say can't be said over the phone. And it has been a long day, painfully so.

"Same here. We're leavin' in the morning. I have business, then you can meet me at my hotel."

"Sounds good." I clear my throat, hoping it doesn't crack again.

"I'd really like it if you told me what's going on."

"Really, I'm fine. Just tired. I need some sleep. Resting up before you get here is probably a good thing." I try to make light with the joke, but it falls flat.

"Get some sleep, and I'll see you tomorrow night."

"Night."

He clicks off the phone, and I toss it onto the bed.

It's way too soon for me and Cooper to move in together like he suggested. I have money in the bank and some stashed here at my house. Maybe I could get an apartment somewhere up there where Cooper is. The problem is: what job am I going to get? There's no way my father is going to tell a future employer that I'm great at my job. He'll be so pissed that I left that he won't see straight. But his options aren't really options.

I can't stay here. My father and brothers have lost their ever-loving minds if they honestly think I'll do either of those two options. Especially when I have serious feelings for Cooper. Now, I'm not naive. This is new, but if I don't follow my heart, then what good is having one? Danger or not, I'm not going to give my entire life up just to do what they want. What about what I want? I have a brain, in case they forgot.

My mother pops into my head.

"Regg, what are you doing?" my mother calls out from the kitchen where she's just finished with an apple pie that I'm dying to eat. It smells so good and fills the house to the point I'm sure the neighbors' stomachs growled outside.

"Not now, Betty."

"Oh no, no, no. You can toss your brass balls around at the club. I gotta take your shit. You come in this home—our home—you respect me as much as I respect

*you. Now, I asked you a question, Regg. My tolerance for repeating myself to you
is as minimal as it is to our kids. What're you doing?"*

She was an iron hand, hard and unrelenting when it came to my
father. She was the dutiful ol' lady at the club, but at home, she was his
equal. When she asked him a question like that day, she expected an
answer. He was simply stopping in to pick up a handgun for Wolf.
Only, Mom didn't know the gun was at the house and it wasn't ours.
Dad was trying to avoid explaining, knowing Mom supported the club
but didn't want the club stuff in her house with us kids being so little.

She would have fought about this with my father. She would have
been his voice of reason. But ever since her passing, he's been losing a
small bit of himself piece by piece. I just didn't think he would ever go
this far with me. I've always been important to him. Well, I thought I
was.

I have to leave. If after talking to Cooper, we don't think it's a good
idea for me to go up there after all, then I'll find somewhere else. My
ties here are to my family and Leah. I can talk to Leah wherever I am,
and my family doesn't seem to want me around the way I am. If I'm
far away from here, then I will be far from danger. Maybe I can carve
out my own happy somewhere else. It's better than these options,
that's for sure.

Getting up from the bed, I grab my suitcases from the closet and
begin packing as pain fills my heart. No matter what happens with
Cooper, tomorrow will be the last day I'm in this house.

The pit of my stomach feels hollow as I drive to work with pretty
much everything I own packed tightly in my car. Pictures, the
memories of my mom and family, those are what came with me. No
furniture. I'll figure it out. Even if I need to find a thrift store to get an
old couch for a while to sleep on, it's better than giving in to my
family's demands.

I have no doubt they think I'll cave, considering I have no one but
them. No extended family, and Leah is my only friend. She still lives
with her parents, so there's no way I have an option there. Her parents
don't like the fact my family is tied to a "gang," as they call it.

My father probably thinks this is my only option. Little does he
know I will give up everything just so I don't have to concede. That's

not how I see my life—trapped in a relationship where the feelings aren't mutual.

I watched my parents. My father adored my mother and treated her like gold. I want that, someone who loves me for me. Not someone who wants me on his arm for decoration.

Why this sudden turn? Is the danger really that bad that it would force my father's hand like this? I don't know, but I hate that it's coming down to these options. The thought of never talking to the only family I have cuts like a serrated knife down my heart and spine. I don't get why he would even put me in this position. Surely, if I move up north, they'll still talk to me, right? I may not be in the club and be "out" as they call it, but I'm still their sister and daughter. That will never change.

The drive to work is short before I'm pulling into the gates. It will be the last time I enter them. The last time I'm waved in openly with no questions asked. At least, that's the way it sounded from my father and brother. *Out.*

Tears sting my eyes, but I push them down. There will be time to cry later, not now. They will not see me upset. My head will be high as I finish everything to the point I can, gather all the numbers needed, and put everything in place for my replacement, whoever that may be. The plan is to go about my day, and at the end, I will go find my family and tell them goodbye. My heart can't take just leaving without saying goodbye.

I didn't get to tell my mom that. No, only her coffin. Therefore, if I can say it personally, I will. If they want to have a relationship with me after all of this, of course I'll welcome it. However, my gut is telling me it will be the end.

Not many are around. When I enter my office, a solace fills me. My mother sat in the chair that I took over after her death. The job was tossed in my lap. Needing something to occupy my time, I snatched it up and ran with it.

Walking over to the wall, a picture of my father, mother, brothers, and myself stares back at me. It was one of my mother's favorites. My father has his arm slung over her shoulder, and us kids are standing in front of them, no taller than her chin. Pulling my phone out, I snap a picture of it then move to the desk.

It hits me that this phone isn't mine. It's actually my father's. Regardless, I'm not giving it back to him right away. I don't have time to go and get another one. I'll worry about that once I get myself settled.

The day goes by in a blur as I get everything in order, even making lists of where to find certain things, like part numbers for the washers or the phone number to the dumpster company. The desk is bare after I remove my three pictures—one of me and my father, one of me and my mother, and one of me and my brothers—and round chap stick. Everything else is Sinister Sons. There's nothing left for me here.

Cooper texted me earlier, giving me his hotel information and stating he told the receptionist that I'd be coming to get a key. It's the only happy that I have for today, and it sucks that the thrilled feeling I felt before is diminished because of my family.

Taking one last look at the office, I grab my bag and go look for my brothers.

Hunter is easy enough to find. He has trouble looking me in the eyes, no doubt knowing my options are limited. He's always had a soft heart, so who knows what this situation is doing to him. But he is the club. He will always side with the club. I need to remember that.

"Give me a hug," I tell him as I walk up to him, arms extended. He gives it back to me, and I relish in his embrace.

"What's goin' on, Bris?" he asks, trying to pull away from me, but I tighten my grasp, trying desperately to keep the tears at bay.

"I love you. Don't ever think that I don't." A dark cloud of sadness surrounds me, soaking me with its rain and clashing me between its thunder.

We've always been close, and it tears me up inside that I'm leaving this way and not on better terms. But, that's life, and I need make one of my own.

This time, he forces be back, gripping my arms and holding me out at arm's length. "What's this?"

"I'm leaving."

"What do you mean you're leaving? You can't leave," he argues, his brows turning down in frustration.

Giving him a soft smile, I say, "I am. I'm not going to become a part of Sinisters. At least, not the way y'all want me to be."

"I can hold them off for a while," he tries.

I've always loved how big his heart is. It feels good, too, that he'll go to bat for me and try to push back a bit. The thing is, I know he can only do so much. At this point, there's not much left.

"I've met someone, and I'm going to move closer to him."

His face changes in a heartbeat, his grip tightening to the point of pain, anger creasing his features. "So, what? You met some dickhead and that's the real reason you're leaving? It has nothing to do with Sinisters?"

"The ultimatum gave me a push. Now let go of me. You're hurting me." The pain isn't really horrible, but I don't like it, either.

He shakes me hard then releases me. I stagger, but keep upright.

"I can't fuckin' believe you. You'll go off and be someone else's whore, but won't stay here with your family?"

My family has lost their minds. Seriously, they all need to be committed or given meds or something.

"This isn't how I wanted to say goodbye." I feel the tears burn the back of my eyelids, coming to the realization that I won't be telling my other brothers or father goodbye because they'll probably have the same reaction. Damn, this guts me, but I have to tell them bye.

"Fuck you!"

"Fuck you back!" I scream, having enough with feeling the pain in my heart. "You think I'm going to become Sterling's ol' lady just so I can stay here and be part of *your* family? Fuck that! That's not an option. And the fact you all thought this is okay is beyond my comprehension! I can't believe you think so damn little of me. Yes, I've met someone. Yes, I want to be with him. Yes, that does mean that I have to leave, but you pushed me to leave a lot sooner than I planned. You, Racer, Stone, Dad, the Sinisters—all of you!"

"What's goin' on?" My father's voice comes from behind me, and my body stills at his authoritative tone.

Pissed? Try livid. He told me not to make a scene anywhere and definitely with anyone around, but fuck it. I'm leaving, so he has no authority. Angry or not, he's just going to have to deal. I just have to get outside these gates, and I'm gone.

Straightening my shoulders, I turn around slowly, knowing he's going to rip me a new asshole and ready to take it.

Then I stop dead.

"Bristyl? What're you doin' here?" Cooper asks, coming from behind a few of his brothers to stand next to my father.

"Cooper," I whisper, not really believing he's here. With my father. At Sinisters'. Holy shit.

"Oh, man, laundromat girl is a Sinister. This is hilarious!" Ryker

119

yells from behind with a huge laugh.

"I'm not Sinisters," I state firmly. "Today's my last day here."

"What the fuck you talkin' about?" My father takes a step forward, and my brother grips my arm, pulling me back to him. The sneer on his face takes me aback.

"Let her the fuck go, or I'll show you exactly how I'll make you." Cooper's tone is rough, edgy, and downright scary. I don't fear him because he would never hurt me, but a chill snakes up my spine as I rip my arm away from my brother.

My other two brothers come in and join the party, along with all the men who look like some of the guys from the Ravage MC, and of course, Sterling. Lord. *What a way to tell everyone you're leaving.*

I step away from my father as he stands by my brothers, who appear in a flash by his side. Cooper's on one side of me, shock written on his face, while my father has anger on his.

"Dad, I'm not staying. You told me what I had to do, and I'm not doing either of those."

"What did he tell you?" Cooper asks, and my face flushes as I turn to him, really not wanting to tell him and all the people around us, but it is what it is. Nothing can change that.

"He said that, in order to stay here with the Sinisters, I have to either become a—"

"You shut your mouth, Bristyl." My father's tone makes me jump and swing my head to his. "That's club business, not for anyone else's ears."

Finger to my chest, I seethe, "I'm not a part of Sinister Sons, remember? You stated that perfectly clear, so me telling Cooper isn't club business; it's *my* business."

"No," my father demands.

Looking my father in the eye, I say, "He said I needed to become Sterling's ol' lady or a whore. I'm not down with either of them."

"The fuck you are," Cooper says, stepping forward and pulling me toward him. He wraps his arms around me and kisses the top of my head, turning us so he can see everyone.

My eyes hit Sterling's, who says nothing, which is a good thing. There is no need to add any fuel to the combustion that appears to be about to happen.

"You're the motherfucker she's leavin' her family for?" my brother clips, finger pointed in our direction.

"Sounds to me like you didn't give her much of a choice. Lucky for me, because we were already talkin' about her comin' to Georgia with me. You just gave her a push. Thanks for that."

"We need to talk," I tell him, not wanting him to think I'm moving up there because my family threw me out. I mean, I am, but there's more to this decision than just this situation. Damn, why does everything have to be so fucking difficult?

"Later, we have a lot to talk about."

My body sags into him, feeling his heat and reassurance. Yeah, we sure do.

"You mean to tell me that my daughter is the one wrapped up in this fuckin' mess?" my father accuses, his eyes going scary dangerous and making my breath catch. This is not the calm, rational father I've known all my life. He's always the rock, the calm. This isn't him. "You've gotta be shittin' me."

CHAPTER SIXTEEN
Cooper

Anger bubbles like lava in my veins. It seems that Bristyl left out a tiny detail about her family. Not that I ever asked her if she belonged to a club, but she should have told me. She will be answering me the why on that one.

As I hold her in my arms, the world seems to center, calm even, with all the chaos around us.

Wolf asked us for a meeting, knowing we were coming down here to meet the Red Devils club. Pops obliged because we do business with him on occasion. I had no clue my woman would be here in a heated argument with her family.

I look her brother dead in the eye. "Fuckin' talk about her like that again, I'll make sure you're ten feet under."

"Who the fuck do you think you are?"

I pull Bristyl behind me, feeling the need to pound this little fucker in the face. "Cooper motherfuckin' Cruz, brother in the Ravage MC, that's who I am, motherfucker. Want me to show you?"

Pops steps in, putting himself right in the situation, as my father and brothers move up around us.

"Get your boy to calm his shit, Regg," Pops orders.

"Hunter, stop," Regg orders.

The asshole takes a calming breath and steps back.

"Your daughter is in the middle of this. Cooper says she's Ravage. Therefore, she is. Our club doesn't work like yours, if those are your rules for your women. Kids are always protected, bein' in the club or not. Not here to tell you how to run your shit, 'cause that's on you. I'm tellin' you where we're comin' from. Bristyl is our business."

"And where the fuck were you when that asshole had his hands on her?" I bark at the brothers and father. "Oh, I forgot, you don't protect your own."

Bristyl grips the back of my cut tightly. "Please stop," she whispers.

"Didn't know it was her!" Regg barks back.

"Find that damn hard to believe," Rhys cuts in. "Unless you have somethin' on them and they wanted to keep you out of it."

"Bingo!" Ryker calls out, and I hear my father chuckle. "We have a winner."

"Don't worry about what I've got goin' on." Her father looks around. "Shit's gonna get real. Those fuckers know who Bristyl is."

"Oh, and now you give a shit?" my father says, putting his hand on my shoulder and giving it a knowing squeeze. "Seems to me you gave up that right."

"Damn straight. I respect your patch and your position, but man to man, she's mine. My responsibility. Mine to protect." I let out a huge sigh, remembering stories Bristyl told me about her mother. It baffles me that this man would say such a thing to his daughter. "How would your ol' lady have felt about this shit?"

Regg's body jerks at the mention of his woman, like he's surprised I know about her.

"From what I heard, she adored her daughter," I continue.

"Fuck you, you little prick." He steps closer, but Pops is between us.

"Wouldn't talk to him like that, Regg. He's got a fuck of a punch. VP of this club or not, he won't back down," Ryker warns.

Bristyl peeks her head around me. "Dad, what you said to me ... what you want me to do, Mom would have never gone along with that. Where'd you go wrong? What's happening to you? This isn't you."

Regg lets out a huge breath, then rubs his hands over his face before tilting it up toward the ceiling. "Fuck!" he yells then picks up a large cement block from the floor and throws it hard, slamming into the hood of a car.

Bristyl jumps.

"Fuck, Dad. My car!" Stone screams.

Regg turns toward his son. "Does it look like I fuckin' care right now?"

Stone takes a step back.

"Go get Wolf. Meeting. Now," Regg orders.

"I can't believe you fuckin' did that to my car," Stone says, walking out of the place.

"Seems we have a lot to talk about," Pops says. He's not kidding one damn bit.

"Guess shit's gonna get interesting. And here I thought laundromat girl was sugar and spice and everything nice," Ryker quips, stepping closer and smiling down at Bristyl. Never once have I wanted to punch a brother for looking at a woman, but that woman has never been Bristyl.

"Cut the shit," I growl.

He throws his hands up in mock surrender, smile still on his lips. "Down, tiger. I'm not gonna take your toy."

My blood boils, but Bristyl giving me a squeeze and me inhaling her flowery scent grounds me. This isn't the time or the place to get into it with Ryker.

The door bursts open, and Wolf walks in with Stone on his heels. "Can someone tell me what the fuck is goin' on here?"

"Seems like my daughter is the cause of Red Devils and their shit," Regg says to Wolf.

Wolf looks at Bristyl, then me, his eyes narrowing into slits. "Care to tell me why the fuck you're holdin' her?"

No, I fucking don't.

Looking over at Pops, he nods. Out of respect for him and Wolf, who is the president of Sinisters, I speak, but I do it so they understand there is no room for discussion on any of this. "Bristyl is mine. I'm takin' her home to Georgia after all this shit is cleared up."

He laughs. "*Yours?* You're mistaken boy."

My body vibrates as anger pulses through me. Respect or not, this fucker will not talk to me like that. Absolutely not. Good thing for him, I've learned control.

"I'm not a motherfuckin' boy. I'll wipe you out and anyone else who gets in my fuckin' way."

Pops steps in front of me and holds up his hand as Bristyl squeezes me again. I look down at her.

"It's okay," she says softly.

Oh, how wrong she is.

Pops speaks, "Wolf, we've got problems with the Red Devils because of shit that went down at Burnout. Bristyl and her friend were the ones we were protectin'. So, that means this is your problem, too."

Wolf laughs again, then looks at Bristyl. "The fuck it is. You decide if you're gonna take Sterling or take us all?"

"Shut the fuck up!" I bark as Bristyl jumps.

"It was you. You told them they had to do it." Her voice starts quiet, but grows in strength. "You told them to give me the ultimatum. You did that to me and my family!"

Wolf continues to chuckle. "All women are good for is fuckin' and makin' babies. Got no other use for 'em. Got no other use for you, except ridin' my cock or someone else's in the club. You're born and bred a Sinister, and that's where you'll stay."

Regg has a hard time looking at his daughter, and she calls him out on it. Meanwhile, my mind reels from the declaration of this man. He's not going to let her go? This is going to be an all-out fight for Bristyl. One that I will win.

"Dad. Because of him?"

"Club rules, Bristyl."

"Since when?" she asks. "When did he tell you to do this?"

"None of your concern. Now get away from that boy and get your ass over here," Wolf orders.

I push Bristyl back behind me. Yep, I'm fighting my way out of this shit. Fine by me, too. Let's fucking do this.

"She's not going anywhere with you, you sorry excuse of a man." This surprises me because it comes from Regg, who has his gun pulled out and on Wolf.

Holy fuck!

Regg holds his piece steady as I keep Bristyl behind me while angling toward the door. Having no fucking clue what's going on here, precautions need to be taken.

I reach for my piece as I hear my brothers unlock theirs.

Wolf chuckles. "What're you gonna do? End me? Nah, you'll fall in line, just like you're gonna get that bitch of a daughter in line and makin' Sinister babies, and do what I motherfuckin' tell you to do."

"This ends here." Regg pulls the trigger, and a loud crack echoes throughout the room as the bullet hits Wolf right between the eyes. He falls to the concrete floor in a heap.

"What the fuck's goin' on here?" Pops barks out harshly, his gun aimed right at Regg.

Tension runs thick as Stone, Hunter, and Racer have guns in their hands, too. Nevertheless, it's the shocked expressions on their faces that have me believing this was not a planned incident. At least there's that.

Bristyl screams, and I pull her to me, pushing her head against my chest. Hell if I know if she's ever seen a dead body before. I do know it's not something that leaves your brain, and I need to protect her from that.

Regg lowers his gun to his side. "Ain't takin' anymore of his shit. He's not runnin' the club right and was sendin' us down the wrong path. Fuckin' over it. I failed my kid once; I'm not doin' it again."

"What have you done, Dad?" Stone asks in shock.

"Takin' back this club." Regg shakes his head. "You know I didn't like this shit. Didn't want to tell Bristyl that. Yeah, we got shit goin', but fuck, it's all Wolf's fault. I'm over it. We need to clean shit up and get this club back to where it was before Wolf went wrong."

"Is Bristyl in serious danger?" I ask, not really giving a shit about their bonding pissing match. They want to stab their president in the back, that's on them. The fact that we have to be witnesses to it pisses me off because it puts us in something we don't need to be in.

"She ain't safe, but we'll make her safe," Regg says as Bristyl turns her head while I try to stop her.

She sucks in a deep breath, no doubt seeing the man lying on the floor in a pool of blood. "I'm not staying."

"You don't have to leave. Everything can stay the same," Regg practically pleads.

"That's what you don't get. I was already leaving, just not this soon. This"—she gestures between her and Regg—"is broken. I love you, but you made some fucked-up choices that I need to deal with. I get the club, Dad. Mom taught me well, which you seem to forget. But what you almost did ... I can't. I need to build a life for myself. Going away is the only option. If it's not with Cooper, then it's somewhere else. I need to do what's right for me."

I drape my arms around her and pull her back to my chest as I lean down and kiss the top of her head, trying to give her the reassurance she needs.

"I know it's fucked-up. I'm ownin' that shit, but it's done. I'll make sure of it," her father tries.

"The decision is made. My car is already packed with everything I own. The files are all up to date. Numbers and contacts are all on the desk. I'm not changing my mind."

"Fuck." Regg runs his hands through his hair, pain and other emotions playing on his face. I'm happy he feels like shit for what he did to Bristyl. It's the least he deserves. "We've got shit to clean up. Pops, we'll have to do this another time."

"Fine by us," Pops says.

"I'm not givin' you up. You may be movin', but we'll be up there to see ya. Family is goin' back to the way it was, not the fucked-up mess it's become," Regg says.

I feel Bristyl lean into me harder, and I take her weight willingly.

"Let's head out," Pops announces while my father slaps me on the shoulder.

Bristyl pulls herself out of my arms, and I reluctantly let go. She runs to her father, his gun still in his hand, and wraps her arms around him. I don't know what she says to him, but his shoulders sag. She does the same with her brothers, while each one gives me the eye of death. *Bring it, motherfuckers.*

"Come on, beautiful."

She takes my hand, and I get her the hell away from all this shit.

CHAPTER SEVENTEEN

Bristyl

Ryker drives my car while I ride on the back of Cooper's bike, helmet firmly in place. Ryker mumbled something about going to get his bike later, but I really didn't it pay it much mind. As we pull away, my heart breaks a little more. The ride is short to the hotel that's just outside of town. It's a mom and pop shop that's been around for years.

Cooper tells me to hop off and I do, numbness seeping through me. I don't know what to think. It's all a clumped up clusterfuck of emotions at once. I'm pissed at my father and brothers. I'm even more pissed at Wolf. I'm scared to death my father will go to jail for killing Wolf. Not to mention, I saw it. That's a torment in and of itself. The blood everywhere on the floor, just running to the floor drain like it's an everyday occurrence.

Wolf came around a lot back when mom was alive. Over the years, he changed, and I made it a point to steer clear of him. He wasn't a man who liked to have his hands in everything, so he left me alone. It's bad, but I don't feel sad that he's dead.

On the flip side of the fear and anger, I'm happy to have Coop in my arms. Part of me wishes we could just hide away somewhere for a while and block everything in the world out. I know better than that, but a woman can dream.

His warm hands grip mine as we walk up the rickety stairs to the top floor where he opens the door. The smell of musk instantly hits my nostrils. I'm pretty sure the only time this place gets business is when bikers come to town.

Sitting on the bed, I stare at my hands. Cooper has to be pissed at me for not telling him I'm a Sinisters' daughter. I never lied, but I didn't tell him the truth, either.

I blow out a deep breath. "I should have told you about my father and brothers. The reason I didn't is because I liked that you didn't know they were in my life. Every time a guy came around, my brothers would scare them off or beat the hell out of them. We are new, and I didn't want my affiliation with them to affect us. Not that I'm a part of them—they've made that perfectly clear—but ..." I trail off, knowing that I'm rambling, yet unable to stop myself. "I know the life. I know my place. Well, I thought I did. What my mom taught me isn't what has happened to me. Everything is confusing. It's more of a mess because they want me back, and I'm not going."

Cooper kneels on the ratted carpet in front of me, cupping my knees as I look into those beautiful blue eyes.

"No, I'm not happy you didn't tell me, but beautiful, we'll work that shit out. I need to know you're okay after what you saw."

I shake my head. "No, I'm not, but I love my father. He did some fucked up things, but I love him and know him. He wouldn't have done that unless he didn't have any other choice. I don't know how to feel about Wolf being the one to call those shots about my life. I don't know how to feel about a lot of it right now. I need time to process it."

Cooper brings his hands to the side of my face. "You take all the time you need."

When he rises, fear hits me that he's going to leave me. Instead, he pulls me onto the bed with him, my back to his front, his safety and warmth surrounding me.

I let it out. The swirl of emotions that come from the pit of my stomach and roll like a tidal wave all around me. Tears fall, then sobs, then hiccups, and it all continues for much longer that I would like to admit. At some point, I cry myself to sleep.

I wake to voices around me. Soft murmurs, actually. My head feels like I swam in the clouds for a while before it all comes back to me. Everything that was said. Everything that happened. Wolf's opened eyes staring up to the ceiling while blood ran from his forehead.

My body jackknifes out of bed as my eyes fly open, looking around in a panic. Then strong arms are surrounding me. I tug and fight, my senses not clear.

"Shh ... beautiful." The words are soft, and I instantly sag upon hearing Cooper, who pulls me closer to his body. He maneuvers his legs out in front of us, me in between them, his arm wrapped around me, and my back to his front.

As my eyes dart around the room, I see several of the Ravage MC standing in front of me, including Pops, the guy who hit on me at the rally, the scary guy, Ryker, and the guy who helped Leah—Green. Turning my head, I see a couple of other guys, all looking at me intently.

"What's going on?" The question is intended for anyone in the room at this point, but I prefer Cooper to answer.

He doesn't.

"We have a meeting and need to figure out what to do with you," Pops says with a small smile tipping his lip. His long, black beard has some gray mixed in, the same as his hair. His eyes, though, are powder blue and stand out intently. He appears strong, yet under it he looks a bit tired.

"Can't I stay here?" I look over my shoulder at Cooper.

"Yeah, but I don't want you here alone until we figure out what the fuck is going on. We have our own mess to deal with, with the Red Devils. Now we're in a deeper mess until we figure out what trouble Wolf has put you in."

"You really don't think he singled me out or anything, do you? I mean, he wanted me to be part of the club and ... you know." I can't say the words. The thought of having sex with Sterling or anyone in that club makes my stomach roil.

"What do you think?" Cooper responds.

That roil turns more.

"Bristyl, are you okay?" One of the guys who looks a lot like Cooper comes up to me. "Son, she's turnin' pale."

My head feels light. I shake myself clear. No way in hell am I passing out or doing something stupid.

I suck in a deep breath. "Can I please have some water?"

The big guy beside me twists off a cap on a bottle and hands it to me.

"Thanks." Taking a few sips, my equilibrium comes back on track. Focus, that's what needs to be done right now.

The guy smiles, and it reminds me so much of Cooper. "Are you Cooper's dad?"

The man laughs. "That obvious, huh?"

"The smile. It's the same."

The arms around me tighten. "That's my ol' man. Cruz, they call him."

I look at his cut and see it has no other title on it, so his rank is just a member, like Cooper.

"Hi."

These men have to think I'm the most pitiful thing.

"Got some color back in your cheeks," Cruz says, rising. "Coop, you've gotta come. No choice. We can have Ryker, Green, and Jacks stay back with her."

"Babysitting duty?" Ryker whines, and my eyes cut to him.

"I don't need a babysitter."

"Good, because I'm not the sittin' type," Ryker fires back.

"Low man on the totem pole. Left the prospects back at the club," the guy who hit on me at the rally says. His cut reads *Dagger*. Geez, I wonder if that means he's good with a blade. I sure as hell don't want to find out.

"Seriously, you're pullin' that card?" Ryker retorts. He must have balls of steel, because the scary man, whose cut reads *Rhys*, doesn't look happy.

"Not pullin' shit. It is what it is. Get the fuck over it," Dagger fires back.

"Alright, cut the bullshit," Pops interjects. "This is what's happenin'. Coop, you come with us. Derek, Jacks, and Ryker are stayin' here, watchin' your brother's woman. And if you got a fuckin' problem with that, then *we* got problems."

The tension in the room gets thick, so much so that the hair on my arms raise. It makes me wonder how often Ryker has an opinion that the guys don't like and if they're tired of his shit.

"Fine, but I get a shot when we figure out what the fuck's goin' on."

Cooper chuckles behind me, and I wonder what the "shot" means.

A bullet? I don't want to know.

"I'm really sorry. I didn't know any of this was going down. My brother told me yesterday that I was in danger and laid all this at my feet. I haven't had a chance to process it all, and I sure as hell didn't want to get any of you involved."

This has turned into a bigger mess than I ever imagined. Way too much going on and way too many variables at play. Not to mention, if Cooper gets hurt, I may lose my shit.

"Shit happens. We roll with it," Rhys says with a slight grin, catching me totally off guard. Who knew the scary man could actually smile?

"Beautiful," Cooper says, and I turn toward him. "Meant what I told you in the parkin' lot. You're mine. I take care of mine. No matter what the problem, I'll fix it. You're Ravage now, and we don't back down."

I turn in his arms fully and wrap my arms around his neck. Never would I have thought a stupid phone call from a customer at the laundromat would lead to this.

Squeezing him hard, I whisper, "I'm not moving in with you. I'm getting my own place."

To that, he laughs. "We'll see."

"Sorry to break this up." Cruz coughs on a chuckle. "Got shit to do."

Pulling away from Cooper, my heart squeezes for the man in front of me. Who would've thought?

Cooper lays a kiss on my lips as the guys leave the room. "Gotta go. Two of them will be in here with you, one outside."

"Do you really think it's that bad?"

"Don't give a fuck if a rabbit hops by your door, beautiful. These men will protect you with their life."

"Or from an unsuspecting bunny."

He laughs. "Or that. Hopefully, when we're done here, we can get the fuck out of this town."

My heart sinks a little. I thought we would spend some time together alone.

Listen to me. All this shit going down, and I'm thinking of myself? Stupid.

"Sounds good."

He leans down to my ear. "Don't worry, I've got a plan."

Between my legs tingles as the warmth from his breath caresses me.

"You do, huh?"

Cooper pulls away and puts his lips to mine, stealing my breath. "Be back."

The door closes. *You'd better.*

"I'm on outside first," Derek says, moving toward the door. "You kids play nice now." His words are directed at Ryker.

"Yeah, yeah."

Ryker grabs the remote to the television and throws his body on one of the two beds in the room. "Might as well catch up on *Judge Judy.*"

The other guy, who I haven't been introduced to, but they called him Jacks, burst out laughing. "No wonder you don't have a woman. Judy? Are you fuckin' kiddin' me?" Jacks moves to the table, stretching his long legs out in front of him.

"She's gotta sharp tongue," Ryker responds as he flips through the channels. He has dark hair, dark eyes, and tattoos all over his arms and neck.

"One that'll bite your dick off."

"I bet it'll hurt so good," Ryker groans.

"You're fuckin' nuts."

Jacks and Ryker carry on as if I'm not even in the room, and I kind of like it. With everything going on, they aren't giving me anything heavy. Instead, they are lightening the mood. I appreciate that.

"What about *Judge Joe Brown*?" I ask, sitting down on the empty bed, my back to the headboard.

"He's off," Ryker says, still flipping. "He got into some legal shit. Jail or banned or something."

This surprises me. I swear I just watched his show the other day. Maybe it was a rerun.

"Really?"

"Yep."

Ryker finds *Judge Judy,* and we watch her kick ass.

CHAPTER EIGHTEEN
Cooper

"This is what we know," Buzz starts, holding his laptop as we meet in Pops' room. Bristyl is only a few doors down, and I can feel the pull to go to her. Strange, yet not. "The restaurant has a back room. There are two exits. One through the main dining area, the other through the back. Cameras don't show anything, but we all know how well that goes." He's referring to when I was a kid. The brothers told me all about the asshole who shot my mother and tried to take my grandmother. He pulled some pretty twisted shit back then, but he's six feet under now.

"Why, again, are we doin' this shit in a restaurant full of people?" Rhys asks, stretching his arms behind his back. Damn man is still built like a brick shithouse.

"So, we don't kill them on contact," I throw in, pissed at Poe asshole for hurting Bristyl. He'll be lucky if I keep my gun in its holster and don't blow a hole through his head.

"This shit's peaceful. Just a chat to get shit straight. We don't know what the Red Devils have to do with Sinisters, and we don't give a fuck," Pops says. "We get in there, do our shit, and get out. Then we deal with the rest."

We ride out and head to meet the Red Devils.

The restaurant is glowing with lights bursting in every direction. Large windows allow the florescent to glow outside, even though it's still bright outside from the sun. Hell, not even my shades are blocking out this much illumination.

People sit in checkered, black and white booths, with shiny blue tables. Five tables are occupied and, counting the drinks at the tables, there are eight people sitting at them. There are nine cars in the lot and seven bikes. Two waitresses could possibly account for two of the cars, making seven cars accounted for. That leaves two.

A brunette waitress yells out at us to take a seat over by the windows, but we don't listen. Instead, we follow Pops as he leads the way toward the back room. As we go, I clock two people at the grill, getting all my cars in order. Now for the seven bikes.

The hallway leading to the back room isn't as bright as the front, but once we enter the back room, we are bathed in light again.

I clock Poe right off with a smug as fuck look on his face. Next to him is Nick and Len, the other two who were at the rally. We've met the president, Scandal, before. He's older, long beard that he combs straight down, and no hair on top of his head whatsoever. With his stern eyes, most people would be nervous. Not us, we're Ravage. No one fucks with Ravage.

Five other men are in the room. Two of whom I've seen before, three I have not. When we met with Scandal a few years ago, I was just patching in. It was him and two others.

"Pops," Scandal calls out, rising from the long table he sits behind.

His five guys sit beside him, while Nick, Poe, and Len stand behind them. There are seats, so some of the guys take them. I prefer to stand, my father next to me.

My blood hums in my veins as the thought of the mark on Bristyl's leg comes to mind. Even only seeing it when it was red and fresh, there's no doubt in my mind that she had a huge bruise from the fucker.

"Scandal." Pops takes the proffered hand.

Greetings and introductions ensue. Once Scandal introduces Poe and his smile turns cocky, my gut screams for me to put him in his place, or six feet under, whichever comes first.

"Seems we have problems with you boys steppin' in on our business," Scandal begins.

I barely catch myself from speaking, not that I can't, but it's better to listen first, react later. Think smart, always. These types of meetings, it's best to let Pops talk.

"Bristyl is our business."

"Since when? When you stepped into somethin' you shouldn't have?" Scandal retorts.

My nails dig into my palms.

"She's Cooper's. Already put a claim on her."

Scandal's eyes lift to mine, no doubt remembering me. My hair was short then, and my body was not as built, but he's a smart man. Otherwise, he shouldn't be running a club.

"Is that so? Poe here says that he has claim on her."

Poe takes a step forward, placing himself right behind Scandal.

Pops looks back to me. "Well?" he invites. I don't need anything else.

"She's mine. You touch her, breathe on her, look at her—fuck, come within a mile of her—I'll end you." My eyes stay focused on Poe as he cracks his neck in some sort of intimidation move. *Sorry, buddy, that shit doesn't work with me.*

"I saw her first," he says.

I want to ask him how old we are, but again, I wait.

I need to punch him, though. The need to take this motherfucker out is growing so fucking strong, but playing it smooth is my game.

"Not playin' this pissin' match. Looks like you have a problem because she's in my bed and not yours. You don't want to take it, that's your problem."

Poe takes a step forward and leans into the table. "It is your fuckin' problem. I'll destroy you."

My lips tip, but I don't take the bait.

"Tell me what the fuck is really going on here?" Pops speaks when I don't. "Cut the bullshit. What does Sinisters have on you that you went to such lengths to keep it from them. I know this fuckin' place isn't that big. I know what goes on in Florida, so don't tell me there isn't somethin' goin' the fuck on. Get real and get real fast," Pops warns.

"I want Bristyl in the fold," Scandal says. "But from the look of your boy, that isn't goin' happen without some serious bad blood between us. That's somethin' I'm not willin' to fuck with." He looks up at Poe. "It's done."

"The fuck it's done!" Poe barks back.

Surprised? Fuck yeah. Pops would have already had a bullet in my foot, then said, "*Son, you've got another one, use it.*"

"You said she was mine. I'm taking it."

Scandal rises from his chair, fury thumping in his features, along with a tick of his jaw. "I fuckin' said it's done. You back the fuck down!"

"Best way to settle this shit is man to man. Ravage isn't afraid to shed blood. But to spare both clubs, let's have them settle this once and for all, like men—fighting," Pops says. "Cooper and Poe, one on one. No weapons, only their bodies. Last man standing wins."

"I'll beat the fuck out of him, but it's not for my woman. It's because you're a piece of shit."

My father drops his hand on my shoulder, giving it a squeeze. "Son, just do what the fuck Pops says so we can get the hell out of here and home."

I shrug, always up for a good fight. Poe's a stocky sonofabitch and no doubt uses that to go in low. He's a piece of cake.

"Just so we're clear, this is for that dick putting his hands on my woman." I pull off my cut, my gun holster, and my T-shirt, handing it all to my father.

Lean fighting machine, that's what my mother has told me. I love the ease of a gun, but using my body is so much more fun. The blood on impact, crack of bone—all if it spikes my adrenaline, adding fuel to my fire.

"Let's do this," I tell the group of men who've started moving tables out of the center of the room and up against the walls.

The floors are a white marble and will be stained with blood very soon. I need to keep a tab on my feet so I don't slip, but with my boots, it should be good.

Poe takes off his cut, gun, and shirt, giving them to Nick.

Lifting my chin to Nick, I say, "You want some next, it'll be my pleasure. Don't ever go near Leah again."

"Fuck you."

"Fuck you right back."

"Go near Leah, and I'll kill you myself," Green says from the sidelines, his words dripping venom. It surprises me because he normally stays pretty quiet. He's more of a silent but deadly person.

Nick's focus goes to Green. "Try it."

"It's not a threat. It's a given."

Nick huffs and moves away.

Poe makes a stupid-ass production of stretching and cracking different parts of his body. I move to the center and stand there, waiting.

"Is the bitch done dancin'?" Rhys calls from behind me with a chuckle. "Let's get this shit done. I've gotta ol' lady to get home to and fuck."

"You done, Miss Ballerina?" I provoke. It does the trick, too, as he comes at me and swings hard, hitting me square in the jaw, a satisfied smile coming to his face. It doesn't knock me down, and as I lick my lip, metallic invades my mouth.

"How's that, you bitch?"

"That was your given. Now I'll show you what Ravage is made of."

I let loose on the man. Rights, lefts, kicks. The sounds of his bones cracking echoes inside the room as I hear my brothers laughing. It's not their first time seeing me do this. It sure as hell won't be the last.

Blood pours from Poe's forehead, nose, lips, and his right eye is beginning to swell.

With a savage right hook, Poe crumbles to the ground, completely unconscious. Sweat pours from my body, invigorated as hell.

I look at Nick. "I'm ready for round two. That was just my warm-up. Come on, Nicky." Taunting him is a bit much, but whatever. It's the truth. He doesn't want to fuck with me when I'm pumped up like this. The hits just get harder because I can't feel the pain in my knuckles. It all numbs; one punch becomes just like the next.

"Fuck you," he says.

I hold my arms out wide to my sides. "I'm right here."

"Nah, you're not worth it."

"Pussy!" Rhys calls out, then Dagger, and the chanting begins.

All I can do is shake my head and try not to smile too much and bust my lip back open. The blood just clotted.

Getting serious, I tell them all, "Bristyl is off limits to you. You come near her, this is what'll happen to ya." I look directly at Nick. "You stay the fuck away from Leah, too. I mean it."

My father comes up beside me, handing me my shirt. Instead of putting it on, I put my gun holster and cut on. It's too fucking hot in here.

"Scandal," Pops says. "Fuckin' with either of those women will put you in bad with Ravage. Only warning. You keep your distance, no problems with us. We gotta come back down here, it won't be pretty."

"I got it," Scandal says, looking down at Poe. "Someone drag his ass to the corner and throw some water on him." Scandal holds out his hand, and Pops takes it. "On my word, this is done."

"Our word," Pops responds. "Also, whatever shit you got goin' down with Sinisters, our ties are cut. We have no dealing with it. If it gets brought to our doorstep in any way, we'll be back and it won't be fists flyin'; it'll be bullets."

"Understood."

"Our work here is done," Pops says, releasing Scandal, but not before giving him the look that would make any man quiver.

There are lots of stares as we leave, but I don't give a fuck because Bristyl is waiting for me.

We ride in a pack all the way to the hotel. As we get off, Pops announces, "Two hours to get some grub and we're outta here."

Nodding, I take the stairs two at a time up to my door where Jacks sits outside in the chair.

"About fuckin' time. If I have to watch *Judge* fuckin' *Judy* one more time, I'm gonna put a bullet in Ryker's head."

Ignoring him, I bang on the door. "Open."

The door swings open.

"Damn, what's the other guy look like? Dead?" Ryker greets.

Bristyl pushes—yes, pushes—Ryker out of the doorway then stops when she sees my face, her eyes going wide in shock.

"What happened? Are you okay? Is anything broken?"

Ryker laughs. "Those questions should probably be for the other guy. I'm out." He steps outside with Derek after him.

"We're pullin' out in two hours. Get food and ready to ride," I tell them.

"Looks like you'll be ridin' before us," Ryker calls out on the way down the hallway.

He's not wrong.

Closing the door, I pull Bristyl to me.

"Cooper, are you okay?" The concern in her eyes is the only thing that's stopping me in this moment from taking her hard and fast.

"Never been better."

Her worry lines grow deeper.

"Beautiful, let me show you." I crash my lips down on hers, the burn from the cut only enhancing my need.

I'm happy I cleaned my shit up before we got back. Breaker had baby wipes in his saddlebag. Fuck if I know why. They worked, so that's all that matters.

She pulls away abruptly. "I don't want to hurt you."

"Beautiful, never."

Our lips connect again in a sea of passion and lust that fills the dank hotel room.

Pushing her against the door, she gives a grunt at the contact then moans so damn sexily that my cock twitches. When I squeeze her plump breasts, she rips her mouth away from mine, sucking in much needed air. Her groans and mewls bounce off the walls.

"Clothes off … now." The demand in my voice has Bristyl's eyes growing wide, then they spark with lust and desire.

She listens as I toss my clothes from my body, including my boots, which take me a minute.

Bristyl stands in front of the door, her beautiful hair streaming down her body and covering one of those luscious tits. Her knee is cocked as she stands on a tiptoe. It's her face, though, the look that tells me she wants me just as badly as I want her.

Grabbing my jeans, I yank out a condom and rip the foil off with my teeth, spitting the bit of plastic on the ground as I sheathe myself.

The need to be inside her is beyond overwhelming. My cock pulses and strains to find its home. That's what Bristyl is. Coming home.

She comes at me, attacking my mouth and wrapping her legs around my body, locking them behind me. I press her hard against the door and place my hands under ass, gripping her tightly. The kiss becomes a desperation.

"I need you," she whispers.

"Put me in."

Bristyl pushes back just a bit, and then my cock finds the warmest, best place on the fucking planet. She moans as I groan.

"I'm gonna fuck you so hard everyone in this place will hear you."

"Coop—"

Her words are cut off when my hips pull back and thrust up hard and deep. I set a punishing pace as her fingers dig into my shoulders. Her gasps and noises are like music to my ears.

She squeezes her core muscles, and I thrust harder, harder, harder; pounding, attacking, giving us both the perfect blend for pleasure.

"I'm gonna …" She screams my name aloud, her nails biting into my skin and her head flying back to crash against the door.

I give her no to time to recover. Instead, I walk her to the bed and take her without abandon until she comes again, and I follow behind her, my cock findings its release.

Home.

CHAPTER NINETEEN

Bristyl

The drive to Sumner, Georgia is quiet, if you don't count the bikes in front of and behind me. It's a bit much, but I'm ready to start a new life. One that's for me. At the same time, nervousness fills me. Going out on my own—hell, going to a club I really know nothing about. It's all wrapped in a tight ball, but my mother's words ring in my head. *"Live life by the balls, my Bristyl. Some chances are worth taking."* Funny how those words just came to me on the drive.

I've thought a lot about my father and brothers and what happened back at the office. The dead body is something that will never escape my brain, no matter how hard I try. Those eyes staring at me ... My body shivers.

I'm also afraid for my father. He shot a man in cold blood. Going to jail and spending the rest of his years there isn't an option. So many of us were witnesses to the murder. So much here could go totally wrong.

What gets me, though, is my father himself. He thought for sure I'd fall in line, becoming something I'm not, instead of standing up to Wolf in the first place. The politics of a motorcycle club are different, my mother used to tell me. She said they were stricter, and one didn't go against the president unless there was a damn good reason. It scares me, yet I feel like he did it to protect me.

Then there is the sadness that I wasn't a damn good reason for my father in the first place. Or maybe I'm seeing this wrong. None of it makes sense. Why wouldn't he or my brothers have my back? At least try. Or maybe they did. There are many unanswered questions, but I didn't go back to Sinisters before we left. The thought of seeing them again hurt.

Even though they want me back in the fold, the problem is trust. All those years we built it. My brothers always on my case about this or that, pushing guys away from me like I'd get some horrible disease. My father was the same. The why is something I can't get over.

I love them and my hope is after time, after we both get our heads on straight, we can talk and work this mess out. Right now, it's too raw. It's a wound that is fresh, and the pain is still sinking in. One thing I do know is that I don't want to see him in an orange jump suit.

The bikes slow, coming up to gigantic compound. I say that, because it's what it is. This place is bigger than Sinisters. The tall, concrete walls around the place with the fencing and barbed wire make it look like a prison of some kind.

The gates slide open, and I ease the gas slowly, taking in the space. An extremely large building sitting off to the left, also made of concrete. There are few windows, but they are small, horizontal rectangles, instead of normal vertical ones.

There's a huge courtyard, with a fire pit, picnic tables, chairs, loungers, and a massive grill. Then, off to the side of that, there is a monstrosity of a playground that has swings, a slide, monkey bars, climbers, and more. Off to the right is a large garage building with *Banner Automotive* written at the top. This is where Cooper works. Interesting.

In front of the garage is a huge lot with cars, and on the opposite side is where bikes are lined up. The guys park their bikes there, and I follow with my car on the other side. Ryker had his bike, so that left me to drive the Challenger back.

"This is where you live?" I ask Cooper as he comes up to the side of my car. I'm overwhelmed by the size of the place, but a bit more on the way the sunlight shines off Cooper's hair. Damn, that man is sexy. "I mean, I know you have a house with the guys, but this is where you grew up?"

"Part of the time. It's home."

Screams of a child pierce the calm, and I whip around to see where it's coming from. Through the door of the largest building, several older woman and children come rushing out.

A woman with beautiful blonde hair, shorter than mine, comes up to GT and wraps her arms around him, kissing him hard. A teenage girl follows behind, her eyes on everyone, but on one in particular.

"That's Angel, GT's ol' lady," Cooper says in my ear.

A knock-out woman with brunette hair and a body so fit I swear she's in her early thirties moves over to Tug, wrapping him up tight.

"That's Blaze," Cooper tells me.

They have to have a rule here. Guys must be hot. Women must be hotter. I so don't fit in.

"You're back." This comes from a woman with hair so dark it's almost purple. She strolls up to Buzz with a smirk on her face, and he pulls her to him and kisses her breathlessly.

"That's Bella," Cooper informs me.

"Where's Tanner and Mearna?" Dagger asks the woman.

"They're at your house. Mearna said they were doing some art something or the other," Blaze responds.

"Fuck, boys, I'm goin' home to make some art." Scary Rhys claps a few of the guys on the shoulders as he takes off.

Cooper makes introduction, and each of them are very nice and welcoming. What's not welcoming is the woman sitting on a white plastic chair with dark hair and red streaks throughout it. She looks pissed as hell at something; either that I'm here or that the guys are back, I'm not sure which. The way she cracks her knuckles, though, is not reassuring on my end.

Cooper laughs at something one of the guys says, not seeing the woman stand up and come our way. Not going to lie, part of me screams that I should run and hide, that she'll tear me a new asshole and then some. But I refuse. With straight shoulders and head held high, I meet her head-on.

Cooper comes up to my side and puts his arm around my shoulder. A noise comes out of his mouth, but he doesn't finish because the woman speaks.

"I don't like her."

This woman, who doesn't know a damn thing about me, doesn't like me? Anger burns in my belly, and my entire body tightens.

"And why's that?" I ask, although she was addressing Cooper. If she doesn't like me, she should say it to my face, not Cooper's.

"You're bringin' trouble, and we don't need that around here," she replies.

I cross my arms in front of me. "I didn't bring anything to your doorstep."

She laughs. "Yes, you did. You think this shit's over?"

"What do you know about it?"

"That you're usin' my boy to get out of a bad spot with your family," she fires back.

"Mom," Cooper says, shocking the shit out of me.

"This is your *mom*?" The words catch in my throat. It takes me a minute to spit them out.

"Yep."

"Great." I look up toward the heavens, but they have nothing to give me. Guess I'm on my own here.

"She did—"

I interrupt Cooper by putting my hand on his chest. "I didn't use Cooper. Did my family give me a little push? Yes. But I'm not using Cooper."

"Where are you going to live?" she charges, hands going to her hips.

"I'm taking care of it, Mom." Cooper's tone turns a bit harsh. He's getting angry.

"I'm going to take care of me. I have my own money and will get a hotel room until I find a place. The fact you think I'm using your boy means you know nothing about me at all. If you'd taken just a minute to introduce yourself and get to know me just a little bit, you would have seen that I care about Cooper. A lot. Do I want this to work out? Yeah, I do. If it doesn't, then I'll deal. Any way you look at it, I'm not going back to Crest, Florida. So, whether it's here I settle or somewhere else, so be it." By the time I end my little spiel, my breaths are coming in heavy and Cooper's arm around me has tightened.

"Are you done?" Princess asks. I know her name from Cooper telling me during our many phone conversations.

"For now."

"Mom, this isn't any of your business. I'm gonna do what I damn well want. You know this," Cooper tells her, and a small smile tips the corner of her lip up.

"She's got grit and a brain."

146

"No shit," Cooper responds, while I say nothing.

Cruz, her man, comes up to her and wraps his arm around her shoulders. "Calm your shit. He's growin' up. You knew it was comin'."

My heart instantly warms. This woman may not like me, but it's really not for me. It's because she doesn't want her boy to grow up. What she doesn't get is Cooper looks like he's been grown for a while now.

"Sucks," Princess says, her eyes going soft for Cooper. "I wish I could smash you small again."

Cooper laughs. "Don't think that's smart, Mom. You gotta chill, though. I want you to get to know Bristyl. Trust me on this."

Princess sucks in a deep breath so hard her shoulders rise with it. When she lets it out, it's like a big whoosh. A small tear forms in her eye, but she doesn't let it fall. It makes me wonder how my mother would feel about me leaving home and coming here. If the circumstances were different and my father didn't pull what he did and I just left to come up here, how would she have taken it? Would she be happy for me? Angry with me? I just wonder what she would have told me. It makes me sad that I will never know that answer.

Princess takes a step forward and, alert, I keep on my toes. For what, I'm not sure. My gut just tells me to be on them with her.

She wraps her arms around Cooper, and I step to the side as he reciprocates. She whispers something so low I can't make it out, and the curiosity hits me. Then she pulls away and turns toward me, holding her hand out.

"I'm Princess, Cooper's mom. Nice to meet you."

Unsure of what to do, my focus goes to Cooper, who smiles and gives me a small nod.

I hold out my hand and take hers. Princess' grip is tight, and it takes a bit for me not to flinch. "Bristyl. Nice to meet you, too."

"Alright, now that the meet and greet portion of this is over"— Ryker claps his hands hard—"there's some pussy that needs tappin'."

It's only after Ryker's gone do I realize Princess still has my hand. She must notice the same, because we release.

"Come on, beautiful, let's go in. I'm beat and need a bit of shut eye."

Cooper's arm comes around my shoulder as he leads me into the building.

I glace over my shoulder, and Princess gives a small smile then leans into Cruz. Maybe this won't be bad after all.

He leads me through the door into darkness. It's not really dark, but the lights are so dim it can be considered darkness. The smell of stale beer and cigarettes fill the air, but it's a smell I'm all too familiar with. Tables line the area as men and women mingle around, but that's about all I see before Cooper pulls me down a hallway then through a door on the right.

The room is small, but from the small bit of light that comes through a window very high on the wall, it looks clean. The bed is made with a black comforter on it, the floor looks picked up, and there's no laundry anywhere. Hell, even my room at home had clothes on the floor. His room is almost spotless.

"Are you a neat freak?"

He laughs deeply in his gut. "Fuck no. I'm sure this was my mom." He nudges my arm. "Probably didn't want you thinkin' I'm a slob."

"She clean your room a lot?"

"Nah, not since I was a kid. See? She likes ya."

"That's debatable."

He wraps me in his arms, his face a hair's breadth from mine. "I like ya."

I grip his shirt tightly. "Good 'cause I like you, too." I kiss him hard and wet.

My body sizzles against his, and before I can blink, we are both naked and fully *liking* each other.

CHAPTER TWENTY
Cooper

"I'm not staying here," Bristyl argues with me. It's damn cute she actually thinks she's going to win this one.

"Just until we find a place we like."

"Until *I* find a place *I* like," she retorts, making me smile.

"*We*, beautiful. We're gonna get a place close to here, and *I'm* gonna pay the rent."

Bristyl's face turns a shade of red that reminds me of a tomato, except her head seems like it's about to explode. Her hands in fists, she glares at me. It's fucking adorable.

"You are *not* paying my rent, Cooper Cruz. I am more than capable of paying for my own and don't need a sugar daddy. Now, I'm gonna look at apartments." She storms out of my room at the clubhouse and down the hall. I follow, because that's the direction we both need to be going. All the while, a smile plays on my lips.

Rounding the corner, I hear, "If you're done with him, I'll take him. He's an amazing lay."

Tina. *Fuck.*

A scream echoes as Tina falls to the ground in a heap.

Bristyl steps back, covering her mouth, eyes wide as she looks from me to Tina, who is screaming on the ground with blood pouring out of her nose. Bristyl's breaths begin to deepen as I move up to her and wrap her in my warmth.

"What did I do?" she wonders, her words muffled behind her hands.

Suddenly, applause breaks out in the clubhouse. It starts small and ends up in a roar, with whistles and all.

Bristyl looks up at me. "What's going on? Who is she?"

Tina rises to her feet. "You bitch," she spits out, lunging for Bristyl.

Instantly, I block her, and Tina's pissed off eyes come to me. "What, she your ol' lady now?"

"Yep."

"What?" Bristyl asks, her hands finally falling from her mouth.

"You're my ol' lady," I respond naturally, then turn back toward Tina. "Spread that shit. No one comes near me or Bristyl."

Tina's face turns sour as she storms off and out of the clubhouse.

"We seriously need to talk," Bristyl says as my father and Pops come up, each wrapping me in a one-armed hug then stepping back.

"About time," my dad says.

"Whatever, old man."

My father takes a shot to the shoulder. It stings, but I never let it show.

"Next one, we're in the ring."

My father laughs. "Maybe tomorrow. Right now, I've gotta get home to my wife."

He leans down and wraps Bristyl in his arms. She stares at me, wide-eyed, her arms out at her sides awkwardly. When I lift my chin, she puts her small arms around my father, or tries to. She only gets about three-fourths of the way.

"Welcome to the family," he says.

"Cruz, I don't—"

"Roll with it." Once the words leave my lips, I get her glare from over my father's shoulder.

"Give me some of that," Pops says, and my father releases her as Pops steps up. "The way you're breathin' fire, you'll be a good match for our boy here."

"Pops …" I warn, hating being called a boy more than anything, even from our president, which he knows and which is why he's doing it with a smile.

"I know, I know. Welcome in the fold." Pops gives Bristyl a squeeze on the shoulder, then turns toward me. "Son, you've turned into a damn fine man. I'm proud of ya." Pops wraps me in his arms, giving me a very brief hug, then walks off.

"Cooper, we need to talk—like now," Bristyl says, her hand on her hip, foot pointed out. "I mean, I just punched someone I don't know. That's not me. I don't hit people. Then this whole business with the ol' lady—"

I toss her up over my shoulder and head back to my room, having heard enough of her yapping.

"Put me down!" She smacks my ass.

"Beautiful, fuckin' love it when you slap my ass." My hand connects with her ass hard, and she screeches as we enter the room.

I kick the door shut then toss my woman on the bed and lay on top of her, my weight pressing her into the mattress.

"Cooper, you did not just do that."

"Beautiful, I did. Get used to it."

She begins to sputter words, but I put my finger over her lips. She glares, but stays quiet.

"Told you I wanted this. One thing you gotta know about me is, once I make a decision, I stick with it. You're mine, and there's no going back from that." Only then, do I remove my hand.

"Do I get a say in any of this?"

A chuckle escapes my lips. "As long as you say what I want."

She tries to wiggle, but I have her captured. "You weren't an arrogant jerk on the phone or when we met."

"Never had a reason to be, but this is me."

"I don't like it." The twinkle in her eye tells me she's not being truthful.

"Yeah, you do."

She shifts again. "What do you mean, I do?"

My thigh is rubbing the heat between her legs, and she lets out a sexy as hell moan.

"Your body tells me so. It's your brain we need to get on board."

"Cooper, I didn't come up here for you to take care of me. This is exactly what your mother accused me of doing. That's not the intention. If we do this—*really* do this because I want to—then we're equals. We talk about things before decisions are made. We go fifty-fifty on everything that comes our way."

"I get where you're comin' from, but beautiful, gotta tell ya, certain things, I'm not budgin'. I pay for the rent on the house we get." She starts to argue again, and I shake my head. "I mean it. This is not negotiable. I take care of you. Now, you can pick out whatever the fuck you want in the place, and I'll live with it. I leave grocery money on the table, you get the food. That's my idea of fifty-fifty."

"What, so you're going to let me actually talk now?"

Smiling, I answer, "Sure, beautiful, just know some things a man won't let his woman do for him."

She lets out a very heavy breath like the weight on her shoulders is too tough to bear. This makes my gut twist. She doesn't need to stress about this. I got it, and she needs to know that, but I let her say her peace.

"Cooper, this is going way too fast for me. Yes, I care about you very much. Yes, I want to be with you. But just jumping into a place together and you taking over paying the bills ... That's just not how it works."

"Says who? You got some instructional manual?" *'Cause I sure as shit don't.* They don't exist.

"No."

"Didn't think so. We do this the way we want. I want to take care of you. That's the man I am inside. I don't want to run your life, or tell you where to get a job, or no, you can't. Hell, I couldn't give a shit if you paint our place pink, though it would suck. We're doing this, and we're gonna make it right."

"Don't you think this is warp speed?" she whispers.

I roll off her and pull her body up to mine, our chests inches apart and feet tangled. "This is an eternity compared to my parents."

"Oh, come on. An eternity? Exaggerate much?"

I chuckle at her quick tongue then peck her on the lips. "My father held a gun on my mother the first time they met."

She sucks in a deep breath. "No way!"

"Yep. They exchanged some words, and it got a bit heated. He claimed her right then and there, on the spot, and didn't look back."

Her eyes widen in surprise. "You're shitting me."

"Do I look like I am?" A lone hair brushes against her forehead, and I swipe it off.

"Holy shit, that's crazy."

Shrugging my shoulder, I ask, "How'd your folks meet?"

"At a party. My mom came to the club with a friend of hers. She met my dad, and the rest was history ... I never thought of that before."

"Life has opportunities come and go. It's if you take them and make them what you want, that's the key." *And you, Bristyl, are my opportunity.*

"When'd you get so smart?"

"I'm me. Take me as I am."

"Arrogant ass and all?"

As answer, I crush her lips with mine. She responds instantly, our tongues warring as we move. She threads her fingers through my hair, then farther down to pull the tie out. Pushing her on her back, my hair falls over both of us, putting a shield around us, all the while our lips take from each other.

The heat in the room begins to turn up as I roam her body, grabbing her tits and touching every inch of her. Her lips rip away from mine, and she gasps for breath.

Trailing kisses down her neck and behind her ear, she squirms relentlessly under me. With one hand, she pushes at my chest, while she holds me in place by my hair with the other. She doesn't know if she's coming or going. Me, I know she's coming.

Reaching down, I make quick work of unbuttoning her jeans and reaching below the fabric. It's a tight fit, but I find her clit and begin stroking. The little nub is hard, but I want it pulsing and throbbing, begging for release.

"Cooper." Her gasps are music to my ears.

I slow down the pace and strum it slowly, lifting her shirt and kissing her waist. Using my tongue, I lick around her belly button, then down to where my hand is, stopping and moving back up. She clutches my shoulders, her nails digging in.

"You're gonna come so hard that everyone in this fuckin' clubhouse will hear you scream my name."

She whimpers, "Please."

"Not good enough." Releasing her, I pull off her jeans and underwear, tossing them to the floor. She helps with her shirt and bra.

As she lays in my bed, blonde hair splayed over my pillows, all I can think is, *this is mine.* She is mine, always. I want this vision to be there every morning when I wake up and every night when we sleep. This right here.

Lust, desire, passion, and so much more plays behind those eyes. I'm going to dig it all out of her.

I kneel on the bed, grasp her hips, and pull her pussy up to my face. She's at an awkward angle, resting on her shoulders, but she manages. I support her all the way, taking the pressure off.

Her taste explodes in my mouth as I eat, and eat, and eat, making sure to stay away from her little nub. Without placing my fingers inside her, she doesn't have enough to get off. Her cries only make my dick harder.

Opening my mouth, I take her entire pussy between my lips and suck hard.

"Oh, God!" she screams, clutching the bedding in her fists.

When I pull away and step away from the bed, her head pops up. "Don't stop!"

The laugh bubbles over as I strip down my clothes and grab a condom, holding it in my hand. "Lips on my cock."

To my utter pleasure, she moves quickly to the edge of the bed, then to her knees before me. Her eyes flutter up to mine as she grips my cock hard. I jolt from the pressure, then let out a moan. Damn, that feels good.

I watch with avid fascination as her tongue darts out, and she licks the underside of my cock from base to tip, then swirls the top. It twitches, making her smile. Then her lips surround me, and my knees buckle just a bit.

Beauty. That's what this is. True beauty.

She fits me as far as she can, using her hand to help. Her suction is perfect, and the way she uses that damn tongue ... hell.

Pulling away abruptly, her eyes meet mine. "Bed, now," I tell her.

"Is that so?" she taunts, rising gracefully slow to her feet. "Maybe I want to suck you off." She brings her fingers to my lips, tracing them seductively.

"Don't give a fuck. My dick. Your pussy. Now."

Hell, I've resorted to only short sentences as I slip the condom on my painful cock.

She falls to the bed, and I follow right behind her, kissing her. In only seconds, my cock is inside her, and her back arches as she tries to pull away, but I hold on tight. I have one mission here ... Okay two, and I will succeed in both.

She spreads her legs apart, and my cock bottoms out inside of her as I hit her pelvic bone over and over. Her body trembles, and she's right there, right on the brink. I slow, and her eyes flash up to me, anger lighting them.

"What are you doing? Move!"

I move my hands to each side of her face, making sure I have her full attention. All the while, my thrusts are leisurely.

"You my ol' lady?" With the question, I push in hard and still.

"Cooper!" she cries, but it's not good enough. Not loud enough.

I go slow again, building her up.

"Answer me." I push in hard again and still. Her pussy clenches around me, and my balls draw up. Holding off the release is difficult, but manageable.

"Please?" Bristyl whimpers.

"Answer." Another slam and still.

When her eyes come up to mine, there's a shine in them that isn't desire.

"I'm yours, Cooper. Ol' lady—whatever. I'm yours."

Music to my ears.

I lean down, kiss her, and then make sure she screams my fucking name loud enough that everyone knows she's mine.

CHAPTER TWENTY-ONE

Bristyl

The moment we pulled up to the home, we knew it was ours. Only taking about a day to get all the paperwork signed, Cooper bought—yes, bought—a ranch-style, three-bedroom, two-bath, with a full basement house about a mile from the clubhouse.

We argued a bit about not buying, but renting. Yet, he won.

Now that I stand in the living room, with a cream carpet and windows along one wall that go from floor to ceiling, I'm in love. The view is remarkable because it butts up to some woods, and there is an acre and a half around us. In my mind, I picture Cooper and me lying on a couch, just watching the woods. Calm. Peaceful. Happy.

I don't know how he got the paperwork done so fast, but what does it matter at this point? The thing that sucks is furnishing this place. Leaving everything back home, I thought I'd get some thrift store finds, but this house is so beautiful, I don't know if I can find the right pieces.

I already texted Leah, giving her pictures of each room. She started planning right away. I didn't have the heart to tell her that there was no way we are designing our kitchen in a fifties diner theme. She can plan, though. It'll keep her busy, then I'll break it to her.

Cooper wraps his arms around my body, pulling me tightly to him. "Saw the way you looked at this place when we walked in. You loved it immediately, no hesitation at all. Now it's yours."

"Ours." The one word holds so much meaning to me.

"Yeah, beautiful, ours. You plannin' on paintin' the walls pink?"

"And if I said yes?" I quirk my brow in question, curious as to how he'll answer.

"I'll go buy the paint."

I slap his chest playfully, getting a sexy laugh from him. "No, I like the slate color on the walls. It brings out the rock in the fireplace. But I would like to put a fresh coat on the place, just to make it ours."

"You got it, beautiful."

"I love it when you call me that."

His gorgeous smile appears. "I love calling you what you are."

"You're too much, Cooper Cruz."

He shrugs. "Nah, I'm just right for you."

He is. He's the perfect combination of everything I could ever want in a man.

Damn. A chance meeting at a laundromat. Funny how something like that can change a person's life. Mine is for the better.

CHAPTER TWENTY-TWO
Cooper

"I got an idea."

The table around me is quiet as all the eyes come my way.

Pops called church early in the day, saying he had some things we all needed to discuss. With everything going on, I haven't had a chance to talk to my dad about my ideas. It sucks because I would've liked his thoughts on it first.

"Let's hear it," Pops orders.

"Business is good. Really fuckin' good. But we need to get the money clean. X and Banner can only take so much, and we're pushing it right now."

"Becs and I were just talkin' about this. Keep goin'," Pops says, strumming his beard.

"I've been doin' a shit-ton of research, but it was Bristyl who slapped me in the head."

"In more ways than one!" Ryker calls out, and everyone chuckles.

"Damn right. Alright, she ran storage units for Sinister Sons. Not only would it be perfect if we should happen to need something like that, but it would be a great income. I'd prefer if we kept it cash only. That way, Uncle Sam keeps his nose out of it for the most part, and we can deposit what we need. But if we have to do credit cards, we could do a few, but leave open a row or so of the units, make up rental agreements, and funnel the money that way."

"What'd we have to do?" Dagger asks.

"Find the land and have a company build the units. The people will come."

"You make it sound easy."

"For the most part, it is. If we vote on it today, I can start looking for places to build that are close to here, but not too close, and get estimates."

"How much?" Becs asks.

"When it's all said and done, no more than five hundred K, depending on the land costs."

"What about security?" Buzz questions.

"That'd be your expertise. We'd need a surveillance system, of course, but we'd also need some kind of key card or code with a door that only opens to that code, which changes monthly. That way, we don't have to babysit it all the time."

"And what about rental agreements?" Tug throws in from across the room.

"Bristyl had a phone where people could call. She'd have them meet her at the office to sign the papers. If we let her set up shop in Banner, she can do that from there. That way, people stay out of our shit."

Banner Automotive is on the property, but has a separate entrance that is highly monitored.

"You've got this all planned out, son?" Pops asks.

"Yes, sir."

He nods in approval. "Let's put it to vote. Yea or nay?"

When the resounding yea's come through, I sit back, feeling damn accomplished. Now the real work begins.

"It passes. Coop, you're in charge of this. Don't let us down," Pops announces.

Damn, that feels good.

"No, sir. Never."

"Alright next order of business," Pops says, garnering everyone's attention. "Talked to Regg."

The mention of his name doesn't make me feel anything. He made shit decisions; that's on him, not me. Even though he's Bristyl's dad, that means shit to me after he treated his daughter the way he did. I can only hope with Wolf out of the picture, that changes.

"Bristyl has no threats. It was all Wolf's dumb ass. But he's gone.

They have some shit with the Red Devils, but he wouldn't go into detail. Anyway, all is good, and he wants to meet with his kid."

"That's up to her," I respond immediately.

"Understood." Pops turns to GT and nods. "Your turn."

"Had to put Deke in rehab."

My fists clench and unclench at this sudden turn of events.

"He's into heroin and needs to get clean. It's a three-month program. I just wanted everyone to know."

"Sorry, brother," Dagger says, slapping GT on his shoulder. Then we all do the same.

I sure as shit hope Deke gets his act together.

"It is what it is. Now, we just gotta get him straight."

"Tommy's pushing again," Pops interrupts, pulling the attention off GT, whose face shows how upset he is about his son. "I'm pushin' back. No fuckin' drugs run through Ravage. Weed isn't a drug in our book. Anything heavier, we don't touch. Understood?"

We all nod in agreement.

Drugs have never been my thing. Pussy and booze, fuck yeah. Drugs only reminds me of the incubator and how I felt as a kid, seeing her high and out of it. No thanks. Control is a must. You don't have that when you're hyped up on shit.

"That's it. Adjourned." Pops slams the gavel down, and I again hope like hell Deke can pull himself up.

"Beautiful, I'm home!" I call out through the empty space, my words echoing off the bare walls. The place is still pretty empty, but that's changing later today. Bristyl picked out what she wanted, and I got a super-king bed. We both win.

"Hey, I'm just getting ready to make BLTs. You good with that?" she calls from the kitchen as I step around the corner and lean my shoulder against the wall.

Gorgeous. Beautiful. There are no other words to describe how she looks standing in the kitchen, her hair a tangled mess on top of her head.

She wipes her hands on a towel and tosses it over her shoulder. Her baby pink shirt stretches over her tits perfectly, and she's wearing those damn boy shorts that hug her ass so tight that she might as well not put the fucking things on.

She looks up and gives me a soft smile. "Yes?"

Instead of answering, I cross the kitchen, wrap her in my arms, and lift her, giving her no other choice but to throw her hands around my neck and legs around my body. The contact of the kiss electrifies my cock. It pulses and jumps with each rub from Bristyl's hot core. Her kisses are hot, wet, and ready for me. I love that she always is.

Placing her ass on the counter, we devour each other. She brings her hands to my face then threads her fingers through my hair, giving it that tug I love so damn much. Our tongues dance rhythmically in a passion and desire that I never knew existed until Bristyl. Now, I will never lose it. Never.

She throws her head back as my mouth glides down her neck, licking, nipping, sucking a trail to her collarbone. There, I nibble on the soft patch, gaining moans and whimpers from her, while her body is having a difficult time staying still on the countertop.

Reaching up, I grasp her tits, squeezing them hard through the fabric of her shirt— once, twice, three times. Her breathing picks up, and she begins to pant from arousal.

I whip her shirt over her head and unlatch her bra, tossing it behind us. Her hard-budded nipples call to me. Not wanting to disappoint, my mouth latches on one, sucking hard and deeply, while I fondle both of them. Her grip on my hair gets tighter and tighter, only spurring me on to fit as much of her inside my hot mouth.

"Oh, Cooper!" Her cries are music to my fucking ears.

I pull away, and she frowns, making a chuckle leave me.

"Lie back."

When she complies, I pull those tight-ass, little shorts off her body, tossing the scrap of fabric. The lips of her pussy stare back at me, glistening and plump.

"Open wider," I order, and she spreads her legs straight out then to the sides, making the sexiest looking V with her legs up that high.

Not needing an invitation, I dig in, attacking her pussy. The taste of her bursts inside me as I suck down every drop she gives. Her legs fall, leaving her feet to rest on the side of the counter.

"So much fuckin' better than a BLT, beautiful."

She shivers as I get back to work, wringing not one, not two, but three orgasms out of her just from my mouth. By the time I pull back and rise over her, she's breathless, eyes closed, and utterly sated.

I unbuckle my pants, drop them, and sheathe my cock. Pressing inside of her, the warmth of her pussy surrounds my aching flesh.

"Cooper!" she cries out as my hips set a pace that makes us both start to sweat.

I have to grip her hips to keep her in place from the punishing thrusts. Over and over, my cock twitches and strains. My balls pull up tight as a tingle forms from my spine.

As Bristyl tightens even more around me, I burst inside of her just as she screams out her release. The air around us is hot, and I have to brace myself against the counter for a moment to get my bearings.

Fuck, she's the best lay I've ever had, and the only one I'll have from now on. Damn, I love this woman.

Pulling out of her, she instantly closes her legs and jumps down from the counter. She wobbles a bit, but regains herself quickly.

"Wow, that was a welcome home."

Reaching down, I pull my pants up over my hips, my covered dick hanging out. "Beautiful, it's just the beginning." I lean over and kiss her hard.

Damn. Now this is the way my life is supposed to be.

"I've got an interview at the grocery store and that little hardware store tomorrow," Bristyl tells me as we lie in bed, waiting for sleep to consume us.

"Got somethin' for ya."

She lifts her head and rests her chin on my chest as I look down at her.

"What's that?"

"Ravage is going into the mini-storage business, and I need you to help me with it."

"You want to give me a job?"

"The club will."

"This feels a bit like déjà vu."

I have no doubt that it does, but there is one big difference.

"The difference is, you're my ol' lady. Mine. Good or bad, up or down, we deal with it together. You know your shit when it comes to this, and we need your knowledge. Yes, Ravage will pay you, and pay you well. We're working out all the details now."

"Aren't you afraid this will end—you and me? That we'll get sick of each other or something?"

"Nope," I answer straight. "You're the only woman I've ever wanted to sleep next to. You're the only woman I've went out of my way to see. You're the only woman who makes me laugh in a way I didn't know possible. You're it. I'm it. We make this work no matter what."

"I'm falling in love with you," she whispers.

I smile. "Damn good thing, beautiful, because I'm already there, and that's where this is going. The forever."

Her eyes widen at my words, and a small gasp leaves her lips. "You do?"

"Yeah, beautiful."

She climbs up my body, plants her lips on mine, and shows me exactly how much she loves me, too.

CHAPTER TWENTY-THREE

Bristyl

"I miss you," Leah says through the phone.

It's been a little more than three weeks since I left Florida.

"Miss you, too."

"Sure, you've got McHottie up there. I bet he's keeping you nice and busy." She laughs, a sound that I miss. Like having someone to talk to, do my nails with who's not a testosterone-filled male.

"Yeah, he does. You should come visit."

"I'd love to. My parents will throw a hissy fit, but whatever."

"So, what's new?"

The conversation with Leah is nice, familiar, and enjoyable. Her stories about second chance romances and a new phone call prank that their friends set them up on are entertaining. She can always make me laugh.

After getting off the phone, I look around our new home. It's beautiful. The dark slate walls on some of the accents, the beige on the others, and the rock fireplace give this room such a warm, happy feeling. Add in the brown sectional couch and two recliners with end tables, and it's perfect.

Cooper and I fought over them. Well, not really fought. I wanted to find used; he refused. I wanted to buy them; he refused. It led to another one of our discussions that ended up with him fucking me senseless and me giving in. It's our way though, and I love it.

I love him. So lucky how that all works. I wish my mom were here, though. If she could see the way Cooper and I are together, she would be happy for us. Happy for me. For us. I can feel her deep inside me like a warm hug.

Letting those thoughts out of my head, I sit at the computer and get to work. In the last week, Cooper and I have found two different potential spots for the mini-storage. It's my job now to figure out which is going to give us more bang for our buck.

This whole job is fun. Not only do I get to work with Cooper, it's exciting seeing something come from nothing and being in on the planning. We have a meeting with Pops and the club in a few days to go over all the plans. My ducks will all be in rows before that.

The knock on the door has me pulling away from the kitchen table where my laptop sets. Going to the door and looking out the peephole, my breath catches.

Princess. Holy shit. What's his mother doing here?

Cooper and I have spent most of our time together here at the house, giving us some time to get in our groove. We haven't been at the clubhouse much; therefore, I haven't seen any of the Ravage MC.

I suck in a calming breath, put my shoulders back, and open the door, my heart beating so fast it's ready to jump out at any moment.

"Hi," I greet on a smile.

"Hey, we're gonna talk," she demands.

While that doesn't sit right with me, she is Cooper's mother, so I give her that respect.

"Sure, come on in." I back away from the door, and Princess glides in, taking off her sunglasses and looking around the place.

"It's nice. Can tell you did it, though. Coop can't coordinate anything."

I chuckle. "Thanks. That's why the shirts with jeans. Can't go wrong with that."

We move to the living room, and an awkwardness settles around us. We ended on good terms. Well hell, maybe not.

She takes a seat on the couch, and I opt for the chair.

"So, what's going on?" I ask.

She smirks. "Direct. I like that." She shakes her head. "You need to come around the clubhouse with Cooper. You're his, and you need to make that statement to the club. *Everyone* at the club."

"Oooookay," I say, not really knowing what else to say.

"Coop told me about your momma. I'm sorry about that, hon. It sucks, but you seem to have a good head on your shoulders. After all, Coop's damn picky, and he wouldn't make that mistake." I sit, listening and taking it in. "In Ravage, you need to make your presence known as being Cooper's. There are a lot of greedy bitches out there who will do anything they can to get their hooks in him." She laughs. "I heard what you did to Tina. That shit's priceless."

Hell, I still can't believe I punched a woman.

"You need to show everyone that you're by your man's side every step of the way. That means coming to the club on the back of his bike. That means helping out in the kitchen when we have get-togethers, which I will tell you is often. You're the next generation of the Ravage MC ol' ladies, and you set the precedence for everyone who follows you. Younger, older, it doesn't matter because you're in. They will look to you for guidance."

"But I don't know much. My parents kept me pretty far away from the club life. I only went to Sinisters for barbecues and stayed mostly with my mother."

"It's not like that here. You'll see when we have our first one. You chip in, help out, and let your man know that you have his back at all costs. You also make sure you know when is enough, especially in front of the brothers. Ravage has a code they live by. They respect us, but we are not members of the club. Your man is, and you need to show him that respect."

Memories of my mother float through my head. I can hear her saying those exact words to me when I was young and learning.

"My mom told me the same thing, but you saying them helped me remember."

She places her hand on mine and gives a little squeeze. "Life is tough. There'll be ups, and there'll be downs. It's how you handle them that makes all the difference. You love my boy?" I nod. "And that's what matters. Love. Love is what binds us all together. We have that, we're strong. We lose it, we're weak. Ravage is never weak, and we never back down. You need to make sure that your position is said loud and clear. And bitches like Tina, you'll take down if needs be."

"I get it. We'll make it a point."

"Good. Now tell me about these units and what kind of money they could bring in."

On this, I blow out a breath, get my computer, and begin to explain. Two hours later, we are laughing as Cooper walks in the door.

"Mom? What's up?" he asks, tossing his keys on the table by the door and coming my way. He wraps his arms around me and pulls me tightly to him.

"Just hangin' out with your woman. But I'd better get going." She rises from the chair, grabs my hand, and squeezes. "You'll make a good ol' lady. Stick with me, and I'll teach you everything you need to know."

"Mom, I don't think that's a good idea at all."

Princess puts her hand on her hip and looks up at her son. "I know you're joking right now because, if you're not, I'm going to have to lay you out in front of your woman."

He laughs. "That's the shit I'm talkin' about. Bristyl's good; let's keep her that way."

Princess laughs. "You should have gotten a job as a comedian, boy. Good? You're around Ravage now, everything is going to open her eyes." She moves toward the door. "See you two at the clubhouse next Sunday night for dinner. Oh, and maybe we'll take a go-around in the ring."

My breath catches. She can't be serious.

Cooper gives me a squeeze as I answer, "We'll be there, but not in the ring."

"We'll see." Princess leaves.

"Care to tell me what that was about?" he asks.

I turn in his arms. He's so damn handsome he takes my breath way knowing he's mine. All mine.

"She's just helping me out and giving advice. I'm not sure about the ring thing, though."

He chuckles. "She'll teach you a thing or two. Who does she want to beat the hell out of now?"

I laugh because that comment doesn't surprise me in the least. "No one. She's a good woman. I like her."

"Good, since you'll be seeing a lot of her."

"Yeah." Lifting on my tiptoes, I plant a kiss on his lips. "Glad you're home."

"Me, too." He lets out a deep breath. "But we gotta talk about somethin'."

"This is the same thing as Leah telling me her harebrained idea of meeting that jerk at the rally. If it's bad, Cooper, I don't wanna hear it."

"Your dad."

This stops me.

"What about him? Is he hurt?"

"No, beautiful. He wants to talk to you, and I really think you should."

It makes me nervous, which is confusing. I thought we would talk about anything else. Now, everything is messed up.

He's sorry, and I get that, but it doesn't change what he tried to do. My heart can't take any more breakage from my family. At the same time, it hurts not having my father and brothers in my life. It's almost like reliving the pain of losing my mother all over again, only now I have the power to do something about it. Forgiveness comes easier when you lost someone so precious to you.

It's time. He reached out, and I'm ready to close this door so I don't have to live in the past any more.

"I'll call him."

"No need. We're headin' down tomorrow."

My eyes widen in shock. "What?"

"He called the clubhouse and asked if we'd come down. He apologized to me and said he wants to do it with you in person. And your brothers want to talk to you."

"Wow." It takes me a moment to gather my thoughts. It's so sudden, like *bam,* in my face, but it's all good. "Okay, that's fine. I can do this."

"Beautiful, you can do anything you put your mind to." He leans down and kisses me. His lips are the softest thing I ever want to touch mine for the rest of my life.

CHAPTER TWENTY-FOUR
Bristyl

"Why am I so nervous?" I ask Cooper, wringing my hands for the hundredth time as he comes back to the truck with the key to our room.

We are in Crest at one of the chain hotels, and I can't stop fidgeting. My body is a tight wire, ready to snap and zap everything and anything around me. He's my father. There's no reason to be nervous, yet I can't help it. Those feelings of never belonging and him wanting to push me to do something I didn't want to, they ride me hard. They pull me to a place I don't like. Nevertheless, I'm a grown-ass woman, and I will do this.

"Because he's your dad. I can still go with you, Bristyl. You don't need to go alone."

I suck in a breath, hoping it will calm me. It does a little. "No, I need to go to him on my own and do this. And tomorrow, we'll go to breakfast as planned."

We get out of his truck, and Cooper leads us to the room. After pulling myself together, it's time to face the music.

"I'm gonna sleep for a bit. When you get back, you can take me to dinner."

I laugh. "I thought the guy was supposed to take the woman?"

"Beautiful, you're from here; you'll know where to get me a steak."

I stand up on my tiptoes, hand on his chest, and kiss him. "You got it. I'll only be a couple of hours."

"You'll be fine. You need to call me when you get there and when you're leaving." He wasn't too happy about the plan to let me go on my own, but this is something I need. I want my father to tell me what's going on. I want to hear from him and him alone. Having Cooper there may influence what he tells me. It's time to woman up and get this shit done.

"I will."

He smacks my ass on the way out, the door clicking behind him.

Driving his truck is fun as hell. It's a huge four-by-four, and I have to jump to get in the thing. Makes me feel like I can run over just about anything and everything in my way.

When I'm waved into the gates of Sinister Sons, my brain fills with memories. Some great, and some bad of recent.

I can still feel Wolf in this place as I drive up. I shake my head quickly to forget. Wolf deserved what he got. I just wish none of us would have been there to see any of it.

The door opens, and my father stands by the side of it. My pulse picks up, and I swear my heart is going to jump out of my chest.

"Baby girl, I'm so damn sorry," he says as I jump down from the truck. He then envelops me in his arms, and tears form in my eyes. When he kisses the top of my head, my body shakes. Then, when he pulls away from me, his hands don't leave my arms. "I fucked up. Bad. I gotta live with that. Never did I want that for you. Never. And I shoulda put an end to it as soon as it was brought up. It's over now. No one will ever ask something like that of you again."

I can only nod, too afraid to speak and have my voice crack.

"Love you so damn much. Only ever wanted the best for you. If that's not in Sinisters, then so be it. But you're my baby girl."

Blowing out a deep breath, I ask, "It was all because he said so?"

My father shakes his head, let's go of me, and runs his fingers over his mustache and down his face. "Come." He directs me over to a set of picnic tables that I frequented a lot during my time here on lunch breaks. We sit, him across from me.

"Can't tell you a lot."

I nod again in understanding.

"But, yeah. Wolf wanted you in the fold. He pressured me to get you in, and that's my mistake."

"You had to know I'd never do anything like that, Dad."

"Part of me hoped you wouldn't and would get the hell away from here." He looks down at the table, then at his hands. "Things haven't been right around here for a while, but I'm in charge now, and I'm gonna make it right. All of it. We're going back to the way it was. The way it should be."

"That's good. Stone, Hunter, and Racer need that, Dad."

"You need it, too."

My eyes drift off to the distance, lost in momentary thought. "Not here, though. I decided that I need to carve a piece out of life and make it my own. Not what you want or anyone, but what I want. I want to be with Cooper. He's part of the Ravage MC, so that means I'm part of them."

"But, baby girl, you're doing the same thing that was asked of you with Sterling."

My eyes bore into my father. "No, it's not. The difference is that I love him, Dad, and he loves me. There's more to life than a title. Love without it, there is nothing." A funny feeling washes over me like the sun got a little bit brighter for a moment. My mom. *Thanks.*

He sits back. "Got it. He treat you good?"

"The best."

"He'd better."

An unusual silence comes over us as my brothers come to the table. They're not loud and rowdy like always. They're more timid, and as twisted as I may be, I like that they are. It shows me that they know they were wrong.

"Sorry, Bristyl." Racer pulls me up from my seat and wraps me in his arms. "Didn't want to tell you that shit. Didn't want you anywhere near any of it. I'm so damn sorry."

I wrap my arms around my brother. "Thank you. I needed to hear you say that."

"You forgive me?" he asks, pulling back and looking in my eyes.

"We'll work on building that bridge we had together. It'll take a while, but we'll get there."

Stone pulls me in, and then Hunter, all saying the same things. Then we sit at the picnic table, and it's as if a switch has been lifted. My brothers go back to their ornery selves, and my father busts their asses for it.

When it's time to say goodbye, I feel so much better.

I turn the truck over, and a calmness comes over me. We're going to be okay. It will take some work, but we'll get there. I love them, they love me, so it will work.

I pull my phone out, ready to call Cooper, when my phone rings and Leah's name comes up.

"Hey!" I say cheerfully, ready to tell her that I'm home and we need to meet up.

"Come to my house now." The phone disconnects.

Without thinking, all thoughts of Cooper and phone calls gone, I race. Yes, I drive like it's a race to my friend. Confusion fills me. Leah needs me, and that trumps everything.

Swinging the door open at Leah's parents' house, I barge in, searching for her. It's not like her to call me like that and then not answer her phone right away. We've been friends for way too long to keep one another on edge like this. We talked on the phone just yesterday about me coming here to see my dad, and everything seemed fine.

"Leah!" I call her name, just as I hear a scream come from far away. It's Leah's scream.

Where the hell are her parents?

Following the voice, I run full-throttle down the hallway, and that is my first mistake. My father and brothers taught me to always watch my surroundings. Be aware of the people and things around you at all times. Unfortunately, when Leah screams and now cries, all reason leaves me.

Reaching her bedroom door, the air and blood leave my body as shock takes over. Leah is lying on her bed, hands tied to the headboard, feet tied to the footboard, spread wide. She's not naked, but that's the only good thing, because she's black and blue on just about every part of her body and cuts line her beautiful face as the blood mixes with her tears.

It's the man in the room, though, the one with the filet knives and bloodied knuckles, who gets my full attention. Len, the quieter one from the rally, has the scariest look on his face. It's blank, void, cold.

"About fuckin' time you got here." He slices Leah's arm, and she screams.

"Stop! What are you doing?"

"Want her to die?"

174

Shaking my head, I answer quickly, "No!"

"Then you come with me. And bitch, you fight me, I'll gut you. Then I'll come back and gut your friend. I may have to fuck her, too. All this shit is gettin' me hard." He grabs himself with the knife so close I wish he would nick his dick as Leah's blood wipes off on his jeans.

"Where?"

He points the knife directly at me, Leah's blood dripping off the tip. "No fuckin' questions. You make a fuckin' sound, I'll slit your throat, and I don't give a fuck who sees me. Got nothin' to lose." His words register, but they don't compute fully.

Len doesn't wait for me to answer, he gouges the knife into Leah's side, blood streaming out as she cries and screams.

"Get away from him, Bristyl!" she screams as he picks up the blade and punctures her again.

"Shut the fuck up, bitch!"

"Okay! Okay! Stop!" I yell, trying to get Len's attention on me and not my bleeding friend. If I can get him out of the house and away from Leah, her parents should be home at some point to get her help. At least, I can make sure she's safe. Fuck!

"I'll go. Come on. Right now."

"Don't!" Leah screams.

Len lifts his fist and punches Leah in the temple so hard her eyes close. She makes a strange gurgling sound, and my fear for my friend heightens.

"No!" I make a move to go to her, but Len grabs me around the arm hard.

He pulls a syringe out of his pocket, and I fight, kicking, hitting, but nothing fazes him. He's ice cold as he slips the needle into my arm.

"What did you give me?"

He doesn't answer as my body begins to feel like it's sagging. The room becomes clouded, and I feel dizzy. My limbs are heavier than normal, and it hurts to hold them up. Resting them on the ground would be a better option. My head goes foggy, and I fight to stay awake, but within moments, it's black.

"Bristyl!" My name being screamed comes through the haze. It feels like I'm drowning, and every once in a while, I can come up for air, yet the pull overtakes me.

CHAPTER TWENTY-FIVE

Bristyl

I can't keep track of the time. My head goes in and out, but the sound of my name, said in that voice—Cooper's voice—pulls me up, and I slowly blink.

It was a mistake to open them. The vision before me is right out of a horror movie, and I'm not one hundred percent sure whether this is a nightmare or reality.

Cooper is in front of me, his hands tied above his head on a hook. They are so tightly strained that every muscle in his upper body is strung out. It looks like each tendon could snap. His feet are barely touching the floor, and a slight sheen of sweat covers his entire body. His shirt is torn and bruises line his abdomen.

How the hell did he get here?

"Bristyl? Are you alright?" Cooper asks.

I sit up, realizing I'm on a dirt floor.

Cooper gives a grunt as something hits him from the back hard, like a crack of a whip. Instantly, I rise, wobbling along the way, but halt when Nick steps out of the shadows, holding a long, leather bound whip that has several long strands on the end each with something sharp. Cooper's blood is dripping from it.

"What's going on?" I manage to get out. My arms are gripped and pulled behind my back as Len stands there, still no expression. The fight in me isn't strong, but I try with no success.

"Little Bristyl," Nick says way too calmly for the situation. He holds his tool like a prized possession, skating his hands up and down the leather rhythmically. "About time you got here. You missed the fun. Here, let me show you." Nick turns and slices the whip through the air, hitting Cooper all over the front of his body, spilling blood.

"No!" I scream and try to fight again. "Stop it!"

"Oh, you want me to stop, huh? Alright, then let's go over here." Nick walks casually to the other side of the room where it's dark. A sconce comes on, and my knees give out. When they do, Len doesn't move his arms and the pain from the angle shoots through me. I stand instantly, trying to relieve it. All Len does is chuckle.

My focus isn't on my pain, though. No, it's on my father. My father who looks almost like Leah did, except he's not strapped to a bed. No, he's bound to a chair, hands behind his back, and feet tied with rope. His head hangs awkwardly, making my heart pump even faster. Poe stands behind him, a baseball bat in his hand.

"Dad!" I scream, fighting my restraints.

His head comes up, his eyes directly on me. "Bristyl?" His voice has a bit of slur. I don't know if they drugged him, like they did me, or if it's from the injuries.

"I'm fine. Are you okay?"

Len takes the opportunity to yank my arms hard, and I cry out.

"Motherfucker, you just wait," Cooper growls.

My father's focus moves to him. "Cooper? What's goin' on?"

Nick walks up to my father and punches him square in the jaw. My dad's head jerks to the side, but he comes back, his focus coming a little bit clearer. His silver mustache is a rust color from his blood.

"Shut the fuck up," Nick spits. "You had to go and fuck up the plan!" he screams, his cool demeanor taking a hike. "This is all your fault!" He points his finger at my father who now has blood running down his face from his head. "You stupid motherfucker had to go and kill Wolf." He shakes his head. "You ruined everything!"

Nick grabs the bat from Poe. He raises it and slams down hard on my father's kneecaps, the echo of crushing bone reverberating through the room.

Tears stream down my face. Screaming doesn't help. Fighting

doesn't help. Len just holds me tighter as I watch the bat come down on my father's other kneecap.

He cries out in pain, something I have never heard my dad do in all his years.

This isn't happening. This can't be happening!

"Please, I'm begging you stop!"

"Oh, you want me to stop? Alright. Then I'll just take this over to your boyfriend." Nick walks over to Cooper as I scream at him.

The swing is massive, hitting Cooper in the gut. Pain etches all over Cooper's face, but only a deep grunt comes from his lips.

"This what you want? Want me to beat on your boyfriend or your dad? Hmm ... Here's a better question for you: which one do you want to live? Because one of them is dying today," Nick asks, and my stomach twists as emotions flood me.

Nick heads over to my father again, and I scream, "No!"

Then he walks over to Cooper, and the same thing happens, over and over. Every so often, Nick will take a swing at one of them while I scream.

I yell. I wail until my throat burns and I taste the metallic of my blood before I swallow it down. The longer I scream, the less I can be heard as my vocal cords strain from the stress.

"Put her in the fuckin' chair, then go deal with that bitch you left," Nick orders Len.

"You said you wouldn't!" My words are frantic.

"I lied." He smiles as he pulls me to a chair. It has metal lock cuffs on the arms that he easily gets my wrists in.

Fighting isn't working.

I kick and hit him square in the chin. He jerks, latches both of my feet, then moves over to Cooper. Silver gleams in his hand.

"Don't!"

Just then, Len sticks the knife in Cooper's leg, turns, and walks out of the room.

"What do you want?" I scream at Nick. "What did we ever do?"

He steps up closer to me. I try to move my arms, but it's no use. They are stuck. Tears stream down my face as the anger begins to bubble in my veins. It's like a switch inside of me that has never been tested before. Even with tears coating my cheeks that have now stopped, I stare at the man.

"Your father killed Wolf. Wolf was going to take over the Red

Devils, and *we* were going to take over Sinister Sons. Your father is supposed to be six feet under, not Wolf!"

It makes sense, but why are Cooper and I here?

"You were our prize. The three of us, not just Poe, we were supposed to have you, and now we will." He leans over and his lips cover mine.

I yank my head back after biting his lip. He pulls back and slaps me across the face. My head whips around until I feel my neck twist. Heat then pain expands like a spider web through my face, but I turn back toward Nick.

"So, who's it going to be? Your daddy dearest, or your boyfriend?"

"You want me to pick who lives?"

"The choice is yours. One of these motherfuckers walks out of here. The other, we bury."

This is fucked up on so many levels.

I look to my left and see Cooper hanging there, his eyes directly on me, fire burning in them. Then I turn to look at my father. His head is to the side and eyes are closed. *Please tell me he isn't dead.*

"Now!" Nick screams.

"Boss," Poe calls. "Len has himself a mess with the bitch. He needs backup."

Nick looks at all of us. "Fine. Hurry the fuck up and get back here."

It's then I realize something. Nick has no intention of killing one of the men I love—yes, love. No, he's going to kill them both, right in front of me so I'll fall in line with whatever his stupid brain has in store. He's fucking with my head about who to choose.

My heart breaks and shatters at the mere thought of losing the two most important men in my life. Memories of my father, the loving, caring man he was when my mother was alive. How he would make sure my shoes were tied before I got on my bike and fixed the scrapes on my hand when I fell.

Cooper. We have just begun, and there's so much more for us. My feelings for him run so deeply it's to my soul. I love him and need him more than my next breath.

"You stupid bitch, answer me!" The blow hits me in the eye, creating an explosion of colors behind my now closed lids.

I scream.

"You motherfucker! You're a fuckin' pussy, hittin' a woman," Cooper taunts.

I want to scream, "*Shut up. He'll come for you, and I need to figure out a way out of this!*" but the pain in my face is too much at the moment.

Instead, I mutter, "You, Nick. I choose you to die today."

The backhand comes down before I can brace myself, and everything goes dark.

CHAPTER TWENTY-SIX
Cooper

That fuckin' piece of shit. He will die, and it will be by my hands. I don't know how the fuck they got me here. One minute, I was sleeping at the hotel. The next, I'm being hoisted into the air. Hell, my body feels like it's been beat to hell and back, but my memories of it don't come.

These fucking assholes are going to pay. Every damn one of them.

Bristyl doesn't know it, but she's been our saving grace. When Len left, it heightened our probabilities of getting out of here alive. My plan was to lure Nick over here, snap his neck, then rush Poe. Since Poe decided to make an exit, that means I only have one fucker to go, and he's a damn moron.

My muscles strain. Not from taking all my weight, but from me holding on and trying not to move. Whoever tied me did a very basic square knot, which is a huge mistake. It took me a bit, and the fucker hit Bristyl twice because of it. Still, she's our saving grace. While she kept his attention, I was able to loosen the ropes.

The burn in my shoulders drives me. The fire in my leg from the stab keeps me aware. When you can't feel pain is when you're fucked. I feel it all, and I feel the rage that comes with these fuckers touching what's mine. They are only fueling the fire.

I'm counting on the adrenaline pumping through my veins to get us out of this fucking mess. I'm not sure how my legs will react once I put weight on them. I've been hanging here for a while, and the numbness has set in.

Nothing is going to stop me, though. Bristyl will walk out of here alive and well.

As Nick walks toward me, my arms give a shake and I will them to stop. Nick can't see the trembling. I need him close to incapacitate him. I'd love to beat the fuck out of him, but we need out of here now.

"You stupid fucker. Had to get involved with somethin' that didn't involve you!" Nick screams, his face turning a shade of red.

His muscles pull tight as he charges toward me, fist ready. Just when he's about to swing, I twist my body and swing myself slightly to the left, letting go of the rope as I do and landing on my jellied feet. Thank God for the fire breathing inside of me.

Nick's eyes look horrified as he begins to reach behind him, where I know he has a gun. I clocked it as soon as he came into the room.

Without a blink of hesitation, I rush him, going directly for his neck and twisting with every muscle in my body.

Bristyl screams as bones pop and break, and I land hard on my side, Nick's head still in my hands. He doesn't move, but I give another yank just to make sure. When I do, his head comes with me, still attached by skin, but not by bone. He deserved so much more.

"Are you okay?" I ask Bristyl.

"Yeah. My dad." Her voice is stronger than before. There was a point during this when I could see a change happen in her eyes. A reserve. A knowing.

Getting up from the floor, my side aches like a mother bitch. I search Nick's pockets and find a set of keys and a cell phone. I unlatch Bristyl, noting the red burns mixed in with blood. Motherfucker. Yeah, he deserved so much more.

Bristyl stands and rushes over to her father while I grab the gun out of Nick's back holster and the phone.

Watching Bristyl untie her father, I make the call.

"Coop?"

"How far out?" I ask my father.

"Only fifteen minutes. Regg called, said there was something suspicious going on with Red Devils. Your tracker was showin' an unknown place. Called you; didn't answer, so we left. Where are you?" He must be in his truck since he answered.

"Somewhere underground. Not far, because I hear cars. I'm finding a way out. Just get here."

"Searchin'," he says. Then I click the phone off.

"Your brother's number?" I ask her as I help untie her father. She tells me as Regg starts to blink, and I start to dial.

"What the fuck?" he asks, looking confused as hell.

"Yeah?" a guy answers on the other end. I really don't give a fuck which one, but I need to know it's a brother.

"This is Cooper. Who's this?"

"Stone. What's wrong?"

"Poe and Len are going to Leah's house right now. Need you there. Take them out—I don't give a fuck—but get Leah away from them."

"What's goin' on?" Stone asks again. I can hear him moving and yelling to his brothers to move it.

"We were taken. I'll explain later. But they're going to kill Leah. Get to her." I disconnect the phone and shove it in my pocket.

"Daddy?"

"My fuckin' legs hurt," he says, looking down at his knees. "Fuckin' hell."

"Don't got a lot of time." I look at Bristyl. "Can you walk?"

"Yeah."

"Good, 'cause I'm gonna need to carry his ass out of here. The calvary'll be here in fifteen."

Regg is a big man, and it fucking kills my ribs to carry him. Not to mention, my leg. Regardless, I pick his ass up, putting him over my shoulder in a fireman's hold.

"How do they know where we are?"

"Tracking devices. All Ravage wear them." I move us toward the door that Poe went out of earlier, then pull the gun from my jeans, handing it to Bristyl. "If it's not Ravage or Sinister, you fuckin' shoot."

She takes it and nods.

I open the door and look around. Nothing. We move down a long hallway. The ground is dirt, walls are concrete. There are so many twists and damn turns in this place.

I shift Regg on my arm.

"Sonofabitch," he growls. "Don't like this shit."

"Get used to it," I groan, every step agonizing.

We reach a door.

"Bristyl, open it carefully."

She steps in front of me and does so as light shines in. Fucking hell, a set of stairs. Thank God. Step by step, we make our way up. Each one is more painful than the last. I feel my vision waver as the pain tries to beat my will. I'm motherfuckin' Ravage; I have a will of steel. We are getting out of this. My resolve pushes me on.

I do a full-out scan of the area. We are at an old church that looks like it hasn't been used in years. Gravestones line everywhere. A fucking cemetery.

I move everyone to a small out-building, not knowing if the other two assholes are on their own or have more.

Regg leans his head against the concrete wall, pain on his face. The normally stoic man looks like his spirit is as broken as his body. He is bloodied and bruised everywhere. He needs a doctor and fast.

"Cooper, how did they know?" Bristyl asks.

"Buzz. He's a technology guy. The tracking devices detect sudden changes in heartrate and body temperature. He gets alerted when it's off. Since he knew I was down here, he probably kept a close eye on it."

"Holy shit."

Motorcycles sound off in the distance, and my attention goes to them. Seeing Pops, I let out a silent breath. Bristyl's safe. We're all safe. Family came. They always do.

CHAPTER TWENTY-SEVEN

Bristyl

My mind is muffled in confusion, each thought taking so much energy. They all just tangle and mingle, not making a damn bit of sense. Voices above me are soft.

Nick has a whip.

The thought startles me awake. I pop up and look around the room, my breaths rushed.

"Calm." Copper's voice comes from behind me, and he wraps his arms around me.

Looking around the space, I see we are in a hospital room, and my father is lying in the bed, not looking happy. My brothers are standing at the windows, eyes on me.

"What's going on?" I ask, quickly piecing the puzzle together. The room. The hurt. The blood …

"You're fine, beautiful. Safe."

I turn toward Cooper, whose body is black and blue. I'm not even sure how the hell he's standing. His gorgeous face is marred with so many cuts, bruises, and swollen that he barely looks like himself.

"Oh, my God." My hand goes to my mouth.

"I'm fine. Doctor's stitched me up."

Not thinking, I burrow my head in his chest. He gives a small grunt, but before I can pull away, his arms are around me.

"I got you. No one will touch you again. I swear it."

"Damn right," my father growls. "Stupid motherfuckers."

I turn back toward my father. "How are you?"

"Busted kneecaps. All the rest will heal." His expression is dark, fierce, and determined. "Motherfuckers."

"Do you need surgery?"

"Yeah, due to go in tomorrow. My blood pressure, or what the hell ever, was bad, so they had to get it under control. Gonna be in fuckin' leg braces," he growls.

I know what that means. No riding his bike. Damn. But at least he's alive.

My head whips back to Cooper. "Poe and Len. Leah!"

"Breathe, beautiful. She's alive and here in this hospital. Green is with her and hasn't left her side. She's beat up and has a few broken bones, but the doctors said she'll heal." This gives me a little reassurance, but I want to see her.

"And the others?"

"Gone," Stone says from the wall.

"What?"

"Gone. You'll never see them again, Bristyl. I promise you that."

"I don't wanna know."

"You're not going to know. Just know you're safe," Cooper says.

Tears fall from my eyes. I can't stop them, no matter what I do. Everything comes out as I fall into Cooper. It's selfish as hell to have him wrapped around me, but I need him. I need him more than I've ever needed anything. My strength.

"We've gotta get you outta here," he tells me.

My head pops up. "I can't leave my dad. I need to see Leah. I can't leave."

"Beautiful, you have cuts they stitched up."

I reach up and feel my face. "How did I not know this?"

"You were pretty out of it, and then they gave you a sedative. Said that if we kept an eye on you here by our father, you could stay in here," Racer says.

"Damn."

"It's gonna be okay, I promise. Everyone is good," Cooper reassures. "You need to rest, though, or they're gonna admit you. Let's go to the hotel and get you rested."

I look at my father. "You're gonna be okay?"

"Of course. Takes more than a bat to get me down."

It's horrible of me, but I laugh. He's right. So damn right.

"Yeah, Daddy."

I'm too tired to fight to stay. My mind is in a fog. I hurt not physically, but emotionally. Nothing like this has ever touched me before. I don't need to know what happened to Poe and Len. I simply find my comfort in Cooper, just how it's supposed to be.

"Go on. The boys here'll keep you updated. Doctors say I'll be fine." The look on his face is one of anger mixed with pain. Damn, this sucks. Royally sucks.

"Okay."

Moving over to my brothers, I hug each of them then walk with Cooper out of the room. I stop mid-step when the Ravage MC men's eyes come to us. They immediately stand.

"What's going on?"

Cooper wraps his arm around me. "They're gonna make sure we get to the hotel. They'll stay outside the damn door and protect their family."

A fresh wave of tears hit as Cooper leads us out and to a new hotel room.

"Will you stop babying me?" my father all but snarls.

One week, and he's already a bear. I hate to see what he'll be like in another week.

"Your new nurse will be here soon. You can't look a mess."

"Bristyl, I don't give a fuck what I look like. I can't fuckin' walk right now, and I have bigger fish to fry besides my damn nurse."

Cooper has been wonderful, agreeing to stay until the hospital and Dad's insurance figured out an in-home nurse for him. One thing I have to say about Sinister Sons is they have damn good insurance. Especially to pay a nurse to move in for twenty-four-hour care. My brothers have been dealing with Sinisters, which leaves little time for them to take care of Dad.

Cooper and I have been staying at my old place, so I've been close to take care of Dad. Meanwhile, my stubborn-ass dad now wants me to get on with my life and live it. Can't say I'm not happy to get as far away from this town as possible.

The replays of what happened that day continue to run in my head. I now understand how Cooper feels when he has his dreams. They take a hold and don't want to let go. Hopefully, once I'm away, they will disappear. I have to be optimistic.

A knock comes to the door, and Cooper goes to answer it. He comes back chuckling.

As I'm about to ask him what's so funny, a woman walks in.

Holy hell. This can't be my father's nurse. She's about my height, dark hair, impeccably green eyes, and a body to kill for. She looks to be in her thirties, maybe. Doesn't she have a family to take care of or something?

"Hi, I'm Bristyl. Are you sure you're supposed to be here?"

She smiles wide, and my father coughs.

"Yes, ma'am. I'll just need a little help bringing in my bags, and we're good to go."

Cooper full-out laughs as I look over at my father who has a shit-eating grin on his face. Guess this is going to work out well, after all.

CHAPTER TWENTY-EIGHT
Cooper

My brother and sister are the first to run up to us. I didn't expect any differently. They've been blowing up my phone, wanting to meet Bristyl. We just needed time together and that's what we did. We needed to heal, and luckily, that is getting better. It's now time to branch out into the family, ready or not.

Nox is pretty much a younger version of me, scary but fucking true. He has a little bit of a darker tone to his light brown hair than me, but his features—no one would mistake him being my brother.

My sister on the other hand, she took after our mother in more ways than looks. Her hair is dark brown, on the verge of black. She's growing up too damn fast, and judging by the skirt she has on, I'm surprised my father let her out of the house.

"Hi! I'm Austyn," my sister says to Bristyl.

In the three weeks we've been MIA, her bruises have turned more yellow, which you can't see with her makeup, even as light as it is. She had nightmares for a while and would wake up in cold sweats. I know those all too well. Once I had Bristyl in my arms, though, mine disappeared. I feared they would return after the ordeal, but I've been lucky. My woman, not so much. They have gotten better, though, and are coming more rarely. With time, I hope hers disappear as well.

"And I'm Nox," my brother adds, and my sister elbows him in the chest. "What the hell?"

"You didn't even let her talk before jumping in with who you are, dumb-dumb."

"Introductions, Austyn. Hello!"

"Alright you two, enough." Their bickering has to stop, or I'm going to have to duct tape them to something and cover their mouths. "What the fuck are you wearing?"

Austyn shivers. It's slight, but it's there. "It's fine." Her eyes dart around. I have no doubt the man they are trying to find.

"Dad see you in that shit?"

Her face turns red in embarrassment. "I'm only wearing it for a little while."

"Change."

"You're not my dad!" she screams, and I chuckle.

"Dad sees you, he'll tan your ass."

Bristyl smiles beautifully at them, interrupting, which I'm grateful for. "Hi, I'm Bristyl. Nice to meet you."

"Wow, you're pretty. Will you teach me how to do my makeup?" Austyn asks with stars in her eyes. It would probably do her some good to learn to be subtle and not slap red on her lips.

"Uh, sure, if your mom says it's alright."

Austyn turns. "Mom!" Then she runs off to no doubt get permission for her face.

I watch as my mother looks at Austyn. She points her finger toward the clubhouse, and Austyn's head goes down. Told her to change.

"You're screwed now. She's not going to leave you alone until you show her everything you know," Nox says on a snort, looking over at me and shrugging. "Seems nice." With that, he takes off.

"Well, that was interesting," Bristyl says as I wrap my arm around her and pull her to me.

"You ain't seen nothin' yet."

My mother rushes up to us. She's been over several times since we got back and has demanded to teach Bristyl how to fight. I couldn't agree more. Bristyl needs to learn to defend herself. Truth be told, I haven't let her out of my sight for long these past weeks, needing to make sure at all times she's safe.

The whole thing was my fault. If I would've gone with her to see her father, I could have prevented it. That eats at me. I vowed it will never ever happen again.

"How are you?" my mother asks Bristyl, and not me, grabbing the sides of her arms softly.

Personally, I'm fine. Had some stiches, but luckily, no broken bones and everything is healing fine.

"I'm good."

"Don't lie to me." My mother's tone turns serious, and I hear Bristyl exhale.

"Really, the nightmares are getting better. I feel fine. It's just in my head. Cooper and Buzz put in a security system that I need an instruction manual to figure out, and that helps at night. My dad is healing well with his nurse." She rolls her eyes.

I have not one single doubt good ol' Regg is doing great with his hot as fuck nurse.

"It'll just take time, but I've got this. I refuse to let it control me or define who I am. And besides, during the day, Cooper and I are so damn busy with supervising the workers for the storage units that I don't have time to think. That's nice. I like keeping busy."

"Well, once those things are up and going, you and are I sparring. I'm going to teach you how to get out of certain holds and the best combinations to use on an attacker. After I'm done with ya, no one will fuck with you."

Bristly lets out a giggle. Damn, that's music to my ears. After not hearing it for a while, I cherish each time she lets it free.

"I'd like that."

"Alight, let's go. You're due in the kitchen."

My mom reaches out for Bristyl's hand, but I pull my woman back to me and kiss her hard.

As she walks away with my mother, an anxious feeling sweeps over me. Logically, I know she's safe with her, but on another level, it scares the shit out of me that she's out of my sight. Everything is going to take time, and I got all of it in the world.

"Son." My father comes up to me and wraps me in his arms. I've always loved how he doesn't give a fuck where he is or what he is doing. If he feels like doing something, he does it. I picked up that trait well.

Once he releases me and steps back, his eyes look hurt. I hate it.

"I'm good, Dad. Bristyl's good. We'll be just fine."

"I'm happy those fuckers got what was comin' to them. Bristyl's brothers are like three of Rhys on steroids. Not sure if they're always like that or if it was just because it was their sister caught up in the mix. Dagger said he saw Rhys cringe once, and you know that motherfucker doesn't cringe at anything."

"Yeah, they're gone. That's all I give a fuck about."

If things would have been different, I would have loved to get my hands on those fuckers just for a little while. Regardless, I trust her brothers and mine to make sure they got what was coming to them. Sometimes in life, you have to know your top priorities, and that is Bristyl.

"Glad to have you home, son. Missed the fuck out of you." While true, we've been home for a couple of weeks, I took some time off from coming to the clubhouse.

I look around the space, watching the kids run and holler. "Deke doin' okay?"

"GT says the withdraws are bad and he's angrier than a motherfucker, but he'll get straight. Let's see if the women are ready for us to eat. I'm hungry as shit."

Entering the clubhouse, laughter comes from the kitchen. One distinctly is Bristyl's. Something on my shoulders lifts at hearing that sound.

"Woman! I'm hungry," my father yells into the back.

My mother throws down a towel and marches up to the bar where we stand. "Good thing it's ready." She tilts up, and my father comes down for a kiss. Instead of watching, my focus goes to Bristyl.

Her and Angel are in a conversation that has her smiling from ear-to-ear. Tanner joins in, and that beautiful sound from Bristyl comes again. Yeah, we're all going to be fucking fantastic.

We eat and enjoy our time together, Bristyl fitting into the fold perfectly. As the sun shines down on us, this day couldn't be more perfect.

"Son," Pops says by the fire pit as I stand there, watching the flames move in the sky.

"Yeah?"

"My office."

Not thinking twice, I follow him and find my dad and Uncle GT already inside, waiting. My first thought is something's happened to Deke. I mean, why else would Pops pull us in individually?

"Take a seat, everyone," Pops orders, going around to the other side of his desk and taking his seat.

"What's this about?" GT asks, his eyes looking utterly exhausted, if not haunted in a way.

"Which one of you is takin' over the club?" Pops blows this question out like it's not rocking the entire foundation we stand on.

From the silence, I can tell it catches my father and uncle off guard as well.

"Gettin' old and need a break. This club is my life, will be my life until my dying breath, but it's time for the pressure to come off my shoulders and onto one of yours. Coop, you're young and not ready, but you're a part of this, and I want you here. GT, you've got a shit storm goin' on."

"I don't think I can right now, Pops. Deke is …" He trails off, rubbing his hand over his face, then looks at my dad. "I'll be your second if you want me, but right now, with this shit storm, I gotta take care of my kids and wife."

My dad leans back in his chair, laces his fingers together, and puts them behind his head. "You really want to do this? I mean, ya got more good years in ya than you think."

Pops nods. "Ma and I have made this club our world and that won't change. But keeping up with everything and making sure money, product, contacts—everything is on point is getting harder for me. I want to sit back, let you boys run things, and enjoy life. I'm still a member one hundred percent, but I want to be in the background more now."

The room again goes quiet. This is such a huge decision. Ravage is an entity all on its own, and I can see how it would be overwhelming, even for a strong man like Pops. In Ravage, the rules are clear. If something happens to the president, the vice president automatically takes over. If the president for any reason wants to step down, they have the right to hand the gavel to whomever they want to serve that spot.

If my father says yes, that means he's the new president after our next church.

"I'm in. GT, you're at my side. Coop, you're on the other."

My startled eyes meet my father's. "Me?"

"Yep. Treasurer, you're handling the money. Everything in this club goes in through you and out through you."

Fuck me. Talk about moving up in the ranks. I know I'm more than capable of doing whatever needs to be done in Ravage.

"Done."

Pops claps his hands together and rises. "You're a good team. You'll do well for the club. I'm proud of you all."

I rise in stunned shock, not letting it show on the outside. A lot just happened in that little room, and no one outside is the wiser.

Bristyl comes up to me, wrapping her arms around my waist. "Are you okay?"

I look down at my woman. "Never been fucking better."

EPILOGUE

One Year Later

Cooper

A scream escapes her mouth as I remove the blindfold I made her wear for the past hour.

"You brought me to see Demon's Wings?"

"It's the group you didn't get to see because of those assholes."

She grips my leather and pulls me to her. "And because of that asshole, I got you." She rises on her tiptoes and kisses me hard on the lips.

Being together for a year hasn't changed the passion or the love I have for this woman. Every time our lips touch, it's that same spark as the first time in that dingy diner parking lot. Every moment with her is better than the next.

I reach around her and yank open my saddlebag. She's already wearing my leather on her back, but I'm a greedy son of a bitch, and I want it all, including my ring on her finger.

I get down on one knee, and Bristyl's hand goes to her mouth in shock.

"Make me a happy man and be my wife."

"Yes!" she screams.

Her hand shakes as I rise and put the solitaire round diamond ring on her finger. Then her arms fly around me and our lips connect.

I had the damn ring for two months now, damn near burning a hole in my jeans. But I wanted to do this, have this memory with her. And I'm happy I did. Only thing I'm not happy about is I didn't drive my truck, so I'll have to fuck her in the bathroom later.

"We're getting married," she says excitedly, staring at the ring. "This is so beautiful."

"You're gonna be mine forever."

"Forever."

BONUS -- DEKE

I fucked up. Majorly. My dad is so damn disappointed in me. I never knew that could hurt so damn much. My mom, all she does is cry. And my sister can't figure out what end is up or down. Me, I'm off the shit and not going back on.

My dad said three months, but it ended up being a year because I relapsed. It won't happen again. I'm staying clean and will fight like hell to stay that way. I'd rather die than let that shit control me and cost me anything more.

The door swings open.

"Deke, what's going on?" Princess asks in a rush, no doubt concerned I'm here. I've only been out for a little over a week, but I can't stay cooped up at my parents' house anymore. I'm over it. I'm over everything.

"I need you to teach me how to fight."

"Why now?" she asks, crossing her arms over her chest.

"Because now's when I need it most."

Bound by Passion (Ravage MC Bound Series #2) Preorder today! Releasing: June 2017

Have you ever wanted something so badly it consumes you?
There is a fine line between needs and wants.

Deke Gavelson has wanted his Ravage cut for as long as he can remember. He's earned it. He was born to be in this club. He's not afraid to fight for his place, either.

Then she barreled into his world, and Deke suddenly desires something more than his rag and winning the next round.

Rylie Hollister has lived through hell and back. Each event makes her the strong, independent woman she is today. Until a bitter underground fighter threatens to turn her plans upside down.

These two are bound by their desires, but oh, how that changes when his intensity meets her passion.

ACKNOWLEDGEMENTS

First and foremost, my sinners. You are the bright spot in my day. Being able to chat with you about the craziest shit possible has given me more than I can describe. Without your support and ass kicking, this book wouldn't have come to life. Thank you from the bottom of my heart.

Chelsea, there is so much I can say, so much I could tell the world, but I'll be nice and just say THANK YOU for being a pain in my ass!

To my wonderful beta readers who took apart this book bit by bit so I could stitch it together to make it perfect—thank you. Suzanne, Kimberly, Cola, and Amy, you are fantastic!!

Terri Anne, thank you for letting me use your Demon's Wings!

Leah, thank you for having a wacky life and sharing it with me.

To my family. You supporting me in what I love is everything to me. I love you.

ABOUT RYAN

Ryan Michele found her passion in bringing fictional characters to life. She loves being in an imaginary world where anything is possible, and she has a knack for special twists readers don't see coming.

She writes MC, Contemporary, Erotic, Paranormal, New Adult, Inspirational, and other romance-based genres. Whether it's bikers, wolf-shifters, mafia, etc., Ryan spends her time making sure her heroes are strong and her heroines match them at every turn.

When she isn't writing, Ryan is a mom and wife, living in rural Illinois and reading by her pond in the warm sun.

Ryan can be found:
Website: www.authorryanmichele.net
Facebook: www.facebook.com/AuthorRyanMichele
Instagram: @authorryanmichele
Twitter: www.twitter.com/Ryan_Michele
Goodreads: http://www.goodreads.com/RyanMichele
Email: ryanmicheleauthor@gmail.com

Other Books by Ryan

Ravage MC Series:
Ravage Me
Seduce Me
Consume Me
Inflame Me
Captivate Me
Ravage MC Novella Collection
Ride with Me (co-written with Chelsea Camaron)

Vipers Creed MC Series:
Challenged
Conquering
Conflicted (Coming soon)

Ruthless Rebels MC Series (co-written with Chelsea Camaron):
Shamed
Scorned
Scarred (Coming Soon)
Schooled (Coming Soon)

Loyalties Series:
Blood & Loyalties: A Mafia Romance

Raber Wolf Pack Series (Available in KU):
Raber Wolf Pack Book 1
Raber Wolf Pack Book 2
Raber Wolf Pack Book 3

Standalone Romances Available in KU
Full Length Novels:
Needing to Fall
Safe
Wanting You

Short Stories:
Hate to Love
Branded

Novellas:
Billionaire Up Romance Series
Stood Up (Coming Soon)
Set Up (Coming Soon)
Picked Up (Coming Soon)
Hung Up (Coming Soon)

THANK YOU!